MORE THAN FRIENDS

A MIDDLE SCHOOL ROMANCE

Once more for Sid & Jojo!

Bill

BILL COLE CLIETT

More Than Friends

ISBN-13: 978-1517586416
ISBN-10: 1517586410

Cover design – Lindsay Cliett
Book design – Lindsay and Jason Cliett

For Sudye Cauthen

Chapter One

I spotted the moving van as I rounded the corner, biking home from baseball practice. Not that I'd miss something bigger than a beached whale. I watched as it parked in front of my best friend's house.

What *had* been my best friend's house. Jason and I'd been fast friends since the dinosaurs died. Until his dad broke up our blood brotherhood a month before we were scheduled to start eighth grade. All for a job in some end-of-the-Earth spot named Moose Breath, Montana.

Sure, we could talk and text, but that's nowhere near hanging out together. I missed Jason's sense of humor most. He said they lived so far out in the woods you had to walk toward town to go bear hunting.

For a second I hoped the van meant Jason's family got fed up without a mall nearby or found they were allergic to fresh air. Wishful thinking! It could only mean someone bought their house and was moving in.

I forgot about it till dinner that night. My eight-year-old brother, Travis, was attempting to make his creamed carrots vanish without actually eating them when Dad brought up the subject.

"I see someone's moving into Jason's old house. Wonder who bought it. Anyone seen them?"

"Not me," I said. "Just the two guys starting to unload furniture."

"Vampires," Travis whispered.

"What?" Dad asked, somewhat startled.

"Vampires," Trav repeated. "You know. They sleep in coffins during the day and only come out at night to drink your blood."

"Have you been watching the horror channel again?" Dad looked from Travis to Mom. "Can't you keep him on PBS? The boy's got vampires on the brain."

She laughed. "You're the one who encouraged him."

What Mom meant was when Trav was a preschooler he'd give you a sweet look and ask, "Can I hug you?" Then he'd pretend to bite your neck with the slurping sounds of siphoning out your red-blood cells. Dad thought it was cute and always let Trav hug him. Weird, yes, but whose little brother isn't a bit bonkers?

My whole family has a strange sense of humor. They always say something silly and embarrass me when my friends are around. Jason's the only one who appreciated it, but then he could be even sillier.

Sometimes I think I'm the only normal one. I've wondered if I got mixed up at birth and placed in the wrong crib. Dad's advice is always, "Lighten up, Joshua."

"They're not vampires," Mom said. "Mrs. Coburn across the street talked to them when they arrived yesterday evening. She said they were very nice."

"See, I was right," Travis claimed. "They came at night. Like vampires."

"Let's hope not," Dad said, always money conscious. "Creatures of the night will drive down the selling price of every house in our neighborhood."

Curious, I asked, "Who are they? Any boy my age?"

"Me, too," Trav chimed in. "I need a new friend."

I laughed. "You sure do. No kid your age will come near you."

"Take that back." He looked at Dad. "Tell Josh to quit picking on me."

"Sorry, Trav, but your last three friends did end up with broken bones after playing with you." I made the mistake of laughing after taking a swig of milk and, unable to swallow, choked and squirted half out my nose before I got myself under control.

My little brother went into his crying routine, trying to make us feel sorry for him. "That's enough, Joshua," Dad said, trying to stop our spat. "You know Travis didn't cause those accidents."

"Sure," I said. "So, it's only a coincidence Trav happened to be playing with them when they got hurt. I plan to keep my distance from the little creep."

"Good!" Trav hollered. "I don't want to get your cooties."

"Yeah? Well, I don't want a broken neck, so keep out of my way."

"Okay with me, butt-face."

"Blubber-brain."

"Spam-head."

"Guys!" Mom interjected. "Do you or don't you want an answer to your questions?"

"What questions?" we asked simultaneously.

"I believe you made recent inquiries concerning the possibility that the moving van might have delivered playmates your age along with sundry items such as tables, chairs, and other household paraphernalia." Excuse my mom. She's an English professor and sometimes thinks it's funny to use more words than necessary.

At least she got us back on track. I enjoy teasing Trav now and then, but we'd argued enough for one night. Besides, I'd used the distraction to scoop up most of my carrots in a paper napkin so I could junk them later in the garbage pail.

"What are the answers?" I asked.

"Yes and no." Mom went from too many words to not enough.

"That answers a lot of questions," I said. "How do they apply to ours?"

"I didn't mean to be cryptic. Yes, there is someone your age, Joshua and, no, there isn't a child your age, Travis."

Trav was disappointed. What with his closest friends laid up in casts on arms or legs, his playtime activities were severely limited. Bosham, the family bow-wow, replaced my brother's little friends, and the poor dog was too old to keep up with an overactive young boy.

"Don't keep me in suspense," I said. "What's this new kid like? Is he normal or a nerd?"

"He isn't a he. He's a she. I mean she's a she." Mom gave me a wink. "And a very pretty she from what I hear."

She, my mom, not the new girl, was playing matchmaker again. Ever since that crush I'd had on her best friend's daughter back in sixth grade, my mother thinks I'm a regular Romeo. All we did was go to a few movies together and hold hands walking around the mall but, in Mom's eyes, we were star-crossed lovers. She sees the world through romance-tinted glasses.

I didn't need Mom's help getting a girlfriend, but I didn't tell her that. She'd ignore me anyway. Besides, baseball took up my after-school time and homework for my advanced classes consumed whatever hours were left.

If a really special girl came along, I knew I'd work her into my life in a heartbeat. All girls looked better than they did a year ago, but I'd yet to cross paths with the right one. I'd know when I did. It's called love at first sight.

Mom's definition of pretty and mine don't often mesh. We'll be in the mall and she'll say, "Isn't that girl beautiful?" and I'll say, "She's alright, I guess." But when I eye a beauty who makes my heart beat faster, Mom doesn't notice her. I pay more attention to curves than she does.

Since I hadn't seen her, I didn't give this new girl in the neighborhood another thought. The Boston Cream Pie Mom picked up from the bakery distracted me. That's what *I* call beautiful!

We couldn't leave the table without Dad's daily joke. A stand-up comic is what he'd like to be if he didn't have a family. I'll give him an "A" for effort, but his jokes usually fall flat. His big smile said he thought tonight's joke a sure winner.

"How many lawyers does it take to change a light bulb?"

Mom played along. "I don't know. How many lawyers does it take to change a light bulb?"

Dad looked expectedly at each of us, building up anticipation for the punch line. "How many can you afford?" He broke up, laughing over his own joke.

When he saw we weren't hitching a ride on his hilarity, he asked, "Don't you get it? The number of lawyers you use depends on how much money you have."

I didn't tell him a joke's not funny if you have to explain it. Instead I said, "Yeah, I get it. That's a good one Dad."

That seemed to satisfy him. As he went to his study to do some paperwork, I headed for the kitchen to serve my sentence at the sink. Mom, Dad, and I rotate cleanup duties. Travis is too young, so he gets a pass. I was happy this was my night 'cause I could dump the yucky carrots without getting caught.

After loading the dishwasher, I picked up the TV remote to channel surf, but Mom asked if I had homework. Remembering Georgie Washington and the cherry tree, I admitted I had a little.

"Work first, TV later," she said, trying to make a command sound like good advice.

It wasn't like I had a lot of schoolwork needing attention 'cause I use my time well and finish much of it during free moments in classes and on the roundtrip bus ride. What I do put off and what faced me that night was algebra.

I couldn't care less about numbers. I'd rather schools teach the first two "R's" and drop the third. Reading and writing are fun, maybe 'cause I'm best at them, while arithmetic is a pain in the you know what.

With an English professor for a mother and a silver-tongued trial lawyer for a father, a facility for words was embedded in my genes. But if I wanted to get into geometry in ninth grade, I had no choice but apply my brain cells to the assigned equations. Not for the last time, I wished a mathematician sat squarely on a branch of our family tree.

On my way to the bus the next morning I slowed down passing Jason's old house, hoping to see the new girl, but no sign of life appeared. Could Trav be right? The sun shone brightly in a cloudless sky. Maybe they were vampires.

Hearing the squeal of brakes up the block, I hotfooted it to the bus stop. I took a seat next to Adam, school smart aleck and my baseball team buddy.

"See a new kid get on?" I asked.

"No. Is there one?"

"Yeah. A girl our age and her mom moved into Jason's old house."

"Have you seen her? What's she look like? Pretty?

"Don't know. My mom says she is."

"Arf, arf," he barked. "That's a sure sign she's a dog. Mom's don't look for the stuff we do."

"For sure! Most likely her mom will take her the first day

to get registered."

"Makes sense. Gonna be at practice today?"

"A tractor couldn't pull me away."

Our bus turned into the long line of the unloading zone. "See you," he said.

"Later."

Pine Lake Middle is a big school, so odds were I'd not spot the new girl, even if I knew what she looked like. I thought the ending bell would never ring and, when it finally did, it sounded reluctant. Racing for my bus, I slid into a window seat seconds before Adam could commandeer it.

He's always excited about something, and right then it was a way to improve his swing. Adam's batting average is better than average, but he'll try anything to improve it. His new ideas usually flop. I told him all he has to do is swing where the ball is, and he asked why I didn't follow my own advice.

Our driver revved the engine, ready for take off, when I noticed a girl I'd never seen before. She had that out-of-focus look people get when they're lost. I saw an assistant principal walk over to her and then point at my bus. She dashed toward it, dropped a book, stooped for it, and made the steps seconds before the door folded shut.

The only seat empty was directly behind the driver since most kids don't want to sit close enough to get caught acting up. The girl glanced down the aisle, probably worried that everyone was staring at her.

She could've ditched that worry 'cause all the kids were

talking nonstop at the top of their lungs. I didn't think anyone noticed her. But I was wrong.

"That's her," Adam said.

"Who?"

"Our new neighbor."

"The girl on the front seat?"

"Yeah."

"How do you know?"

"If her mom brought her to register like you said, then I figure she'd want her daughter to ride the bus home so she'll know the drill for tomorrow."

"Makes sense."

"Your mom was right," Adam said, giving a low whistle.

"About what?"

"The new girl. She's fine."

Adam may be a smart aleck, but he's also a ladies' man with a first-rate reputation for judging the female figure. If he says a girl's fine, she's fine.

I don't always agree with Adam, but in this instance I more than agreed. It took only a moment to scope out this young lady since her assets were obvious—perfect figure (I think I could've put my hands around her waist), short blond hair with the sheen of silk, flashing green eyes, delicate ears, almost translucent, like certain seashells, and pierced with tiny pearl earrings. Her face, easy on the eyes, glowed with a radiance almost blinding. Angelic! I half expected to see a halo floating over her head.

My seatmate might've been a couple of laps ahead of me in

the boy/girl game, but I didn't want his reputation. Adam's a love-them-then-leave-them lover, with a flood of tears flowing behind him. Handsome, tall, blond, athletic, a smooth talker, witty, he used it all to his advantage. I watched him check the lovely lady out. I knew him too well. He'd targeted her as his next conquest.

"At least she's not a vampire," I said.

Adam looked at me like I was far out in left field. "A vampire? Where'd you get that nutty idea?"

"Trav, my dumb baby brother, 'cause no one had seen her in the daytime."

"And I thought my little sister was one run short of a winning game."

"He has vampires on the brain," I explained.

"I don't know about vampires," Adam replied, "but I'll tell you one thing. That girl can bite my neck anytime she wants."

Chapter Two

The new girl was first off the bus. By the time Adam and I disembarked, she'd gotten way ahead of us. Living in the opposite direction, Adam headed home practicing his new swing with an imaginary bat.

"See you at practice," I yelled.

"With cleats on," he hollered back.

I could've caught up with the girl by going into a running walk, and I wanted to. But for the life of me I couldn't think of an opening line. Adam would've flashed his pearly whites and the right words would've flowed like honey, sweet and sexy at the same time.

Curious, I wanted to know her name, where she'd moved from, things she liked to do. I knew it would be mannerly to introduce myself, welcome her to the neighborhood, offer a friendly hand, ask her to go steady. Okay, scratch that last one.

I couldn't pull it off. Truth is I'm shy, and shyness makes me feel like I'm locked in an invisible cage that prevents me from doing and saying what I'd like. I can relax and act silly around my family and friends from way back, like Jason, but strangers are another story. Around them I clam up. Words try to roll off my tongue but trip over the teeth and stick to my lips.

My mom is one of the I've-never-met-a-stranger sort. She can talk to anyone and in minutes know their life history. I'd be embarrassed to ask personal questions, but she's not. It's a gift I wish I had, but I don't. The new girl would have to walk home alone.

I changed into my uniform and biked to the Boys' Club where practice was long and hard, but productive. I even helped Adam improve his new swing. On my way back home I had a brainstorm. If you've ever thought of the perfect thing to say after it's too late to say it, then you know how I felt.

I could've caught up with the new girl, introduced myself, said that her new home was where my best ever friend had lived, that when I saw the moving van the day before I'd thought Jason might be moving back. Then it'd be her turn to introduce herself and say where she came from. I'd walk with her to her house, say I'd be happy to be of help if she needed it, and then wave goodbye. It seemed so simple, but that train had left the station.

Dinner was on the table when I got home. After a quick washing of hands and face and the swipe of a brush across my damp hair, I joined the family. Mom didn't wait to begin her interrogation.

"Tell us all about Eve, Joshua."

"Eve who?" I asked, baffled.

"Eve, Eve Williams, the new girl who moved into Jason's old house."

"Oh," I said, letting this information sink in. "I didn't know that was her name."

"Didn't you see her at school?" Dad inquired, cross-examining me as he would've in court.

"No, and I have witnesses to prove it."

"What about on the bus?" Mom said.

They'd double-team me till I told all, which wasn't much. So I explained how I'd seen a new girl get on the afternoon bus at the last minute, sit up front, and get halfway home before I reached the sidewalk.

"Oh well," Mom said, "you can introduce yourself when you walk Eve to the bus stop in the morning."

"What makes you think I'll be walking her to the bus stop in the morning?"

"Because I told Ms. Williams that you'd be happy to stop by their house and then introduce Eve to all the kids waiting for the bus."

Damn if she hadn't done it again, volunteering me without even asking. What nerve. Was I the only boy with a mother like that? I knew it'd do no good to complain but, if I came across strong enough, Mom might think twice the next time.

In my most mature voice I said, "Why don't you ask first before you make promises that involve me?"

"Don't make a big deal over nothing, Joshua. It's good manners to help a newcomer. Put yourself in Eve's place. Wouldn't you want someone to help you get adjusted to a new school?"

How could I argue with logic like that? When my mom

aims the artillery of manners at me, I raise my hands in surrender. I know when I'm outgunned.

I also knew what it's like being the new kid on the block and starting a new school. It was Jason who helped me fit in when we first moved here. Without him, I would've been lost. Still, I didn't like Mom forcing good manners down my throat. Especially when I knew the right thing to do and failed to do it. If I'd introduced myself to Eve and offered my help, I would've been a hero at the dinner table and not an unmannered brute.

Defeated, I waved the white flag. "I'll roll out the red carpet for her," I promised. "But you know how uncomfortable I am around strangers."

"I'm aware of that, Joshua. Think of it like baseball practice. The more you do it, the better you'll become. Thanks for putting up with your buttinski mother."

"You're welcome. What's for dessert?"

While I devoured a healthy slice of chocolate cake spread with deliciously gooey icing, I suddenly realized Mom did me a great favor. Eve expected me tomorrow morning. She knew who I was and why I was coming. She was no longer a total stranger. There'd be no starting from scratch 'cause my dear buttinski mother paved the way for me. It felt like hitting a homerun.

I left the house earlier than usual the next morning to have plenty of time to stop at Jason's, oops, Eve's house. I wiped my sweaty palms on my pants before Mrs. Williams opened the door, introduced herself, and said she appreciated me helping Eve get adjusted to a new school. Mom must've told her about my love for baseball 'cause she asked me what position I played and how the season was going. She was warm and friendly and, when she smiled, I looked at her teeth. No vampire fangs to be seen.

"Hurry up, Eve," she called over her shoulder. "Joshua's waiting for you."

When Eve appeared, I almost dropped my books. She was more than pretty. She was drop-dead gorgeous. I'd only seen her from a distance yesterday on the bus, but now I had a front-row center seat. I'd never seen a girl so beautiful. My heart paused a moment before it began beating again.

"Hi," she said. "I'm Eve. Thanks for stopping by to help me, Joshua."

Words failed me. I had to say something, but what? Nothing clever popped up, so I fell back on the tried and true.

"You're welcome. Happy to be of help. By the way, the kids call me Josh, only my parents call my Joshua."

"Josh it is then," she said, flashing an angelic smile.

"We'd better go," I said. "I'll introduce you to the neighborhood kids before the bus arrives."

We walked together quietly. When I couldn't stand the silence any longer, I asked, "Where did you move from?"

"Atlanta."

"How do you like Florida?"

"Okay. I haven't seen much of it."

You couldn't call her a chatterbox. I'm not much in the chitchat department myself, but I gave it one more try.

"What's your schedule like?"

Eve reached into a notebook, pulled out a computer sheet, and handed it to me. I noticed she'd chewed her fingernails. I also caught the sweet scent of perfume.

"What a coincidence," I said. "We have the same teachers but at different periods. Our lunch period is the same. Did you bring anything to eat?"

She shook her head.

"Big mistake! Unless you like frozen French fries, raw hot dogs, and sour milk."

That brought a chuckle. "Thanks for the warning. I was too nervous to eat yesterday."

"I'll share my lunch with you. Mom always packs more than I can eat. Meet me at the water fountain inside the cafeteria and we can share my lunch and a table."

"Thanks. That's kind of you."

On that note we reached the bus stop. And not a second too soon, 'cause I couldn't think of anything else to say.

The whole gang was there, curious about the girl at my side. "This is Eve. She just moved here from Georgia. Atlanta. Her mom bought Jason's old house." Then I introduced each kid by name. True to his playboy reputation, Adam put on a show.

"Madam, I'm Adam! That's a palindrome. It reads the same way backwards or forwards. Adam and Eve! We'd make a great couple, as long as you won't make me eat an apple."

All the kids laughed.

Eve shot right back at him. "My name's a palindrome all by itself."

"You'd look good in fig leaves," Adam continued. "Even better without them."

Eve blushed, but Adam didn't notice he'd embarrassed her. He was too busy being the center of attention. Fortunately, the bus saved her from more of his smart aleck remarks.

Adam's behavior disgusted me. Happy to have a good reason not to sit with him like I usually do, I shared a seat with Eve.

"I'm sorry," I said. "You okay?"

"I'm fine."

"It's just the way he is. You'll like Adam when you know him better."

"I get jokes about Eve and apples all the time. I'm used to them."

I believed her, but Adam's remark about how she'd look wearing fig leaves or naked went too far. Even worse, he said it in front of a bunch of kids who might spread the story all over school. I'd have it out with my baseball buddy the next time I caught him alone.

"You know how to get to all your classes?"

"I think so. They gave me a map yesterday. This place is like a maze."

"It's confusing at first, but you'll soon learn your way around."

"I hope so. Thanks for your help, Josh." Walking away, Eve turned and looked back at me. She flashed her lovely smile. Then she disappeared into the crowd.

Her smile touched something deep inside me. Eve was

unlike any girl I'd ever known, and I barely knew her. One thing I did know. I wanted to know more of her.

Adam caught up with me outside my homeroom door. "Whatcha doing, old boy, trying to make time with my girl?"

"Your girl?"

"You bet. Eve and I belong together, like the original Adam and Eve. We're the perfect couple."

I shook my head. "You're unreal, Adam. You meet a girl for the first time, embarrass her in front of kids she doesn't know, and expect her to fall into your arms."

"It's happened before," he said confidently. "Girls like a take-charge guy."

"You mean like a caveman. Hit her over the head with a club and drag her by the hair to your cave."

"Sort of, but more subtle."

I laughed. "You wouldn't know the meaning of subtle if a dictionary fell on your head. You're as subtle as a killer whale."

"Laugh all you want, old pal. I haven't seen you kissing any girls at school lately."

"You haven't seen me sitting in the dean's office, either."

"It was worth every minute of it," he shouted over his shoulder.

What a guy! The first day of school and Adam's lip-locked with Amy Lynne in the middle of the cafeteria where three hundred kids could see them. Our school is pretty strict on PDA, public display of affection, where even holding hands is outlawed. All he got was a warning, so I suppose a French kiss with a hot girl was worth it. And I'd yet to kiss a girl.

I waited for Eve by the cafeteria water fountain as I promised, glad Adam had a later lunch period. I looked forward to our having some time alone, or as alone as you can be in the midst of hundreds of hungry kids. She was a little late arriving, limiting our choice of seats, but we finally found a vacant table by the corner of the stage.

As I shared my ample lunch with her, I realized again how very beautiful Eve was. I wanted to talk but couldn't find the right words. Afraid to say the wrong thing, I remained silent. So did she.

I studied her face at close range. Her look was somewhere between serious and sad. But when she smiled, her whole face lit up. I wanted to see her laugh, even telling some funny stories about our school. As a comedian I flopped, not even getting her to giggle.

What finally got the laugh I wanted wasn't the way I wanted to get it. I'd split my food with Eve and then used the top of my orange-juice-filled thermos as a cup for her to drink from. Trying to drink from the thermos itself was tricky and, tilting it up to get the last bit, juice dribbled down my chin and onto my shirt.

It wasn't a mean laugh. It was a musical laugh. I liked it. I liked it a lot.

She was only amused by my clumsiness and immediately touched her napkin to my chin and patted my shirt dry. I had to laugh at myself and was grateful for her thoughtful attention. Somehow I believed the laugh we shared that day was significant, something to build on in the future.

When the bell finally rang, Eve said, "Thanks for sharing your lunch with me, Josh. And your company."

"It was my pleasure. Want to join me here tomorrow?"

"It's a date. I'll bring some food to share with you."

A date! I liked the sound of that word. Even if it didn't mean going out on a romantic date, it still meant the two of us would be together.

When I went to throw away my lunch wrappings I ran into Amy Lynne and her stuck-on-themselves girlfriends. They thought themselves superior to all the other girls in school. Never gave me the time of day—until then.

Amy Lynne didn't waste any time. "Who's that girl you were sitting with?"

"Eve Williams. She's new. Moved here from Atlanta."

"So, *she's* the competition."

"What's that supposed to mean?"

"Only that she's a fast little worker."

"How so?"

"She's been here two days and already has her hooks into Adam."

"You're crazy!"

"You think? It's all over school she's Adam's girlfriend."

Chapter Three

Adam! I've known the guy a super-sized time and he still surprises me by the stunts he pulls. If word was out that Eve was Adam's girlfriend, it could only be Adam spreading the story. Who else would make up something like that?

I stood there a few seconds, shaking my head, stunned. Could Amy Lynne and her gossip girls really buy Adam's lie? I didn't try to dissuade them. Nothing I'd say could change their minds. I only repeated what I'd first said, "You're crazy." Then I walked away.

I'd done everything Mom asked of me. So, technically, I was free to go my own way and leave Eve to sink or float by herself. But something deep inside wouldn't buy it. She needed a real friend, at least until she got her footing and learned the ropes. More than anything, I wanted to be that friend. Maybe I wanted more than that.

This may sound funny coming from a guy who, a few hours before, was nervous about ringing Eve's doorbell and introducing himself. Now I wanted to be her knight in shining armor, rescuing her from a dragon named Adam and his dragon lady, Amy Lynne. I imagined swooping Eve up on my horse and galloping off to my cozy castle.

I shook my head. "Damn it, Josh," I said to myself. "You're starting to sound like a romance novel."

Maybe Eve didn't need to be rescued, or want to be. She'd said Adam's remarks at the bus stop didn't upset her, so a rumor about being Adam's girlfriend might mean nothing as well. Eve's a girl of few words, perhaps a little shy, but inside I suspected she'd be strong as steel. It made me want to draw closer, to know her better.

I took stock of myself. Adam's tall and handsome while I'm average in height and looks. I'm no hunk, but I'm above average in several sports, baseball being my best. I can chew gum and walk at the same time. I wear my black hair short and my clothes are preppy. Mom wouldn't let me wear baggy jeans and tee shirts if I got on my knees and begged.

At least I measured a few inches above Eve. It's good she didn't wear heels to school, not that any girl did. I thought we'd make an attractive couple.

Where was my imagination taking me? I'd known this girl for barely a day and already thought of us as an item. Adam and I were on the same track. Only he made his feelings public while I kept mine hidden. Thinking about it, I found a bigger difference. I believed in love at first sight. He believed in lust at first night.

Was this a romantic part of me I didn't know I had? Or did I just feel protective? Maybe I'd mixed up jealousy with it. Adam seemed so sure of himself. He got any girl he wanted.

Did I only want to show him up for once by taking Eve from him?

Then I remembered Adam didn't actually have her. His saying so didn't make it so. Still, if Eve ever had a romantic feeling for one of us, I wanted her to have it for me. I didn't like it, but I figured it was probably too early for her to have feelings for either of us. Worse yet, maybe she never would.

Or, maybe not. If Adam and I found her an instant attraction, the same could happen with Eve. It didn't take long to find out. I'd gone to my locker to put away some books during the next class change when I overheard Eve's confrontation with Amy Lynne. I didn't mean to eavesdrop, no pun intended, but anyone within fifty feet could tune in on their conversation.

Directly in front of Amy Lynne, Eve got down to business. Her voice was calm but strong. "Are you telling kids that I'm Adam's girlfriend?"

Amy Lynne didn't expect this direct attack. Before she could decide what to say, Eve continued. I couldn't help but admire her bravery.

"Let me clue you in. I am *not* Adam's girlfriend. He is *not* my boyfriend. The next time you decide to spread a story about me, get your facts straight first. Am I clear? Am I speaking a language you understand?"

Eve said the last two sentences slowly with a pause between each word. Like you'd talk to someone who had limited English or brains. There was no mistaking her tone of voice. She meant what she said—every word of it. Then she walked off without waiting for an answer.

Amy Lynne was speechless. It must've been the first time in her life she was at a loss for words. I stayed a second to catch her reaction, but there wasn't any. Amy Lynne just stood there, not sure what hit her, her gal pals gathered around her.

I caught up with Eve as she reached her classroom. "Whoa," I hollered. "Wait up a minute."

She stopped outside the door. I looked at Eve with admiration. "You're something else. And you sure don't need any help fitting into a new school. You can take care of yourself."

"You're right," Eve said as she disappeared behind the door.

I stood there, shaking my head. I'd thought, since Eve was quiet, she might be shy. I reevaluated that supposition. Not many new kids would stand up for themselves like that. Even those who'd been here since sixth grade would think twice before speaking back to Amy Lynne.

In the locker room I ran into Adam. He was dressing back in from his PE period. Late as usual.

"What's all this talk about you and Eve?" I asked.

"What'd you hear?"

"That you two are an item."

"So?"

"So it isn't true."

"Says who?"

"Eve."

"Where'd she hear it?"

"From Amy Lynne or one of her brat pack."

"What do they know about it?"

"I figured they got it from you."

"And if they did?"

"Then it's a lie!"

"Big deal. It'll be true soon enough."

He finished tying a shoe and was off like a sprinter from the starting block.

I couldn't confront Adam again until last period where we were lab mates in science. "When did you plan to tell Eve she's your girlfriend?" I kept my voice friendly as we slit open a frog.

"Any day now," he said.

"Is that the way you usually work?" I was curious, wanting some clue to the famous Adam come-on.

"Sometimes. It flatters girls to find out I like them before I say anything. It makes me seem a little shy."

"Shy! You? This morning you said girls like a take-charge guy."

"They do," he said, probing around for the frog's heart. "They like a take-charge guy who's also sensitive. You've heard of the strong, silent type? It's what you're silent about that's important. Girls can't get enough of it."

Finding the heart, we began delving into the innards. The stink of whatever they pickled the frog in forced me to hold my breath. It backfired when, finally, I took a deep gasp of air and got a double dose of the overwhelming odor.

"You're not making much sense," I said. "Or am I dense?"

"You said it, not me," Adam answered. "Look Josh, all I'm telling you is girls like attention. They like boys to like them. They want us to be the boss without acting bossy. But they also want us to express our feelings."

"You're saying drag them off to your cave where you whisper sweet stuff in their ears?"

"Now you're cooking with propane. It's different with different girls. You search for the right combination. If one approach fails, try another."

"And you think you've used the right combination on Eve?"

"Who knows. If at first you don't succeed, try, try again. She'll come around, sooner or later, to the spell of my charms."

I looked at Adam in amazement. "What an ego! If you could bottle your self confidence, you'd make a million."

"You must believe in yourself before girls will believe in you. That's enough dating tips for today. Help me get this amphibian reassembled."

We washed up, the ending bell rang, and I walked with Adam to our bus.

"Why are you suddenly interested in Eve? There are plenty of beauties ready to fall at your feet, and Amy Lynne's first in line. Eve doesn't even like you."

"Says who?"

"I heard her tell Amy Lynne you weren't her boyfriend and she wasn't your girlfriend. She made it clear she wanted that story to stop. From the sound of her voice I'd say she doesn't like you one bit."

"She said that?"

"Yeah."

"Rad!"

"Why rad?"

"That means she really does like me. Girls usually say the opposite of what they mean. She'll pretend to put up a fight, but Eve's hooked. All I have to do is be patient as I reel her in."

Adam was confident. I'll hand him that. Given his track record, he knew whereof he spoke.

"You didn't answer my question."

"Why I'm after her?"

"Exactly."

"Because Eve's different. Sure, she's lovely to look at, but there's much more, something special, an extra dimension. I can't tell exactly what it is, but I can sense it."

"A sixth sense?"

"No, a sex sense."

"Is that all you think about?"

He laughed. "Is there anything else?"

"How about baseball?"

"It's not in the same league."

I groaned. "Spare me your puns."

"Okay. You want to know what I see in Eve. I see a girl who might let the right guy go all the way."

Chapter Four

Adam's internal clock never keeps the correct time. It always runs slow. Hanging around him is guaranteed to make you late. So, with a last-minute dash, we reached our bus and squeezed through the door as it folded shut.

I saw Eve halfway back, a sixth-grade girl sitting beside her. Adam and I had no choice but to sit directly behind the driver. I had questions about his last remark in science lab and I wanted answers.

I sure didn't want our bus driver to overhear our conversation, so I spoke as softly as possible, yet loud enough to be heard over the chatter and horseplay of sixty or so students. A bit embarrassed, I asked my first question anyway.

"Adam, have you ever gone all the way?"

He didn't seem surprised. Acted like it was a normal and natural enough question. I would've turned red or died if someone asked me something so personal. But then I wasn't Adam. I couldn't imagine any inquiry that would faze him.

"Sorta," he said.

"What does that mean?"

"Somewhere between yes and no."

"Look, Adam, I don't mean to be nosy. It's none of my business, but the way you seemed so sure about Eve and, knowing your reputation with girls, I, like, well, you know, just wondered . . ."

"It's okay, Josh. I know you're not the kind who sticks his nose in another guy's business. The answer to your question, it's a long story."

I smiled. "I don't have anywhere else to go."

"Okay. You remember Marty, that girl with long black hair in our social studies class last year?"

"Sure. She had a face you don't forget."

"And a body."

"That, too. She moved away suddenly, without a word. Seemed shy. I never got to know her."

Adam gave me a conspiratorial wink. "I got to know her."

"You mean like *really* know her?"

"Yep. Really, really know her."

"Go on. Tell all."

"I sat by her in English. Marty got 'A's' on everything. Our teacher said she had a natural talent for writing. Always had her read her work out loud. So I asked her to help me with our assignments, pretending I sucked at English and needed tutoring."

I couldn't keep from laughing. "You didn't need to pretend much, did you? Have you ever read a whole book or written anything longer than three sentences?"

"I'm not as bad as that. Anyway, I told her I really appreciated her help, which I did. My grades moved up from 'D's' and 'C's' to 'C's' and 'B's.' I saw she liked me and I let her know the feeling was mutual."

"Where'd you meet?"

"Her house. Both her parents worked and didn't get home till 6:00 or later 'cause they had to pick up her baby brother from daycare on the way home. We had the whole place to ourselves."

The bus stopped suddenly, the driver opened the door and looked both ways. All the kids yelled, "No tracks, no choo choo." Under way again, Adam continued his story.

"We got on well together. I'm rarely at a loss for words and she was quiet and liked to listen. After finishing our work, we'd talked about stuff, some of it pretty personal. One day, as I left, I kissed her cheek. Nothing passionate, just a thank-you-I-think-you're-nice kiss."

"Did she say anything?"

"Nope. That meant she didn't mind it. After that, I kissed her each day when she walked me to the door. The kisses got longer and moved from her cheek to her lips. Then we began kissing when we got to her house, before we started our homework. We got into a routine where we'd work, kiss, work, kiss. Get the picture?"

"High definition."

"One day I remembered reading a book my sister left lying around. And don't act so surprised. I've really read a few books cover to cover."

"I didn't say anything."

"Yeah, but you thought it. So I remembered something from the book that might take Marty and me to the next level."

"What book?"

"A novel. I think the title's *Robbie and the Leap Year Blues.* This friend of Robbie's tells him how he got a girl naked. He told her he didn't have any sisters and didn't know what a girl really looked like. And guess what? She undressed and showed him."

"Sounds too good to be true."

"That's what I thought. Then I figured, what the hell, it's worth a try. If I sounded sincere and pitiful, she might go for it."

"I take it she did."

"Everything. Right down to her birthday suit."

"Wow! That's amazing. Hey, wait a second. You've got a sister."

"Marty didn't know that."

"Sneaky. You think she bought your story?"

"I dunno. Probably not. The girl was no ballonhead. I think she wanted to. Maybe thought I'd like her better. Who cares? What matters is she did it. Don't argue with success."

"True enough. What happened next?"

"She put her clothes back on. I should've taken mine off too."

"Would you have stripped?"

"Sure. But she didn't ask and I didn't act fast enough. I could kick myself now."

"What happened next?"

"We went back to making out. Hardly did any homework. Things got hotter and heavier, but she always held back. I was dying to do it. Some days I thought I'd explode."

"Did you ask?"

"Does a teacher give tests? You bet I asked, but she wasn't ready. I didn't pressure her. Then one day she said yes. I don't know what changed her mind. Probably felt frustrated like I'd been from the beginning. Teenage hormones have a boiling point."

"What then?"

"She asked if I had protection."

"Did you?"

"No. I could've kicked myself. I like to carry one, just in case, but my mom found it in a pocket of my jeans when she was loading the washing machine."

"OMG! What'd she do?"

"Flipped out. What do you think she did? Asked me all kinds of questions. I couldn't make my mom believe that most boys carry one around or how easy they are to get. It got crazy when she said I didn't even have a 'B' average. I don't know what grades had to do with it. I felt like asking if it'd be okay if I had straight 'A's.' Instead, I stood there and let her run out of steam."

"Go on."

"When my brother went to college last year I got his bedroom. Tucked away in a corner of the closet he left a box of condoms. All types, colors, flavors, and sizes."

"What'd you pick?"

"Something called a French tickler. The package said it was designed to drive women wild. Sounded good, so I took a couple."

"Did it?"

"Drive her wild, you mean?"

"Yeah."

"I never found out. On the big day disaster struck."

"Like what?"

"With a capital 'D,' like in Dad. We were on her bed and down to our underwear when he walked in. He'd felt sick and came home early."

I tried not to laugh. "I'll bet seeing you didn't make him feel better."

"I wouldn't say that. It seemed to perk him up."

"Did he yell?"

"Like a stuck pig. You'd think he'd never been a boy himself. I was so busy grabbing my clothes and getting out of there I didn't hear half of it. But his tone of voice made it clear my presence was no longer appreciated."

"Weren't you embarrassed?"

"Didn't have time to be. Scared more than anything. I didn't know what he might do. I ran out the front door in my boxers and pulled on my clothes in the driveway. All but my socks. They got left in the rush. Marty could keep them for a souvenir."

"Did he call your folks?"

"Must not of. I would've been grounded for life if he had. The next day Marty's dad put her in a private church school."

"How'd you learn that?"

"Facebook. She hated it, but what could she do? And that was that."

"Lust bites the dust, huh?"

"It's still alive and kicking. Just looking for greener pastures."

"Like Eve?"

"Whatever."

The windows of the bus should've been steamed up after Adam's story. They weren't, but I was. I kept picturing Marty naked. My blood boiled and my heart beat like a bass drum in a military band.

Getting off the bus, Adam headed for home, saying he'd see me at practice. His mind was back on baseball while mine was still on Marty. I couldn't think of anything else.

I wondered if I'd dare pull a stunt like that and decided I couldn't. I wasn't a risk taker like Adam. If I'd been in Marty's bedroom when her dad walked in I would've died on the spot.

"Josh, wait a minute."

I stopped. How had I forgotten Eve?

"Hey," she said. "I want to ask you something."

"Sure. What is it?"

"On the bus, when the driver stops and opens the bus door. All the kids yell, 'No tracks, no choo choo.' What's that about?"

"Wacky, huh?"

"I'll say. Is it a joke?"

"The driver's the joke. Used to be railroad tracks there, but they took them up last year. She's stopped at that spot, looking and listening for trains so long, she can't quit."

“Force of habit?”

“We used to tell her to keep going, but it didn’t do any good. She said something could still come down the old road-bed. One day Adam yelled, ‘No tracks, no choo choo,’ meaning a train can’t run without tracks. After that we’ve shouted it every day.”

“It doesn’t bother her?”

“Guess not ‘cause she still stops. We’d be disappointed if she didn’t. It’s become a daily routine.”

Eve laughed. “It’s kinda weird, but I like it.”

“So do I.” Then I said something I hadn’t planned. “I like you, too. The way you stood up to Amy Lynne and her girl gang was something else. I don’t where I got the idea you were shy.”

“You thought I’m shy?”

“Yeah. You’re quiet and look sorta sad.”

“It doesn’t have anything to do with shyness. It’s something else.”

All I said was, “Oh.” Adam would’ve asked what that something else was, but I couldn’t.

Neither of us said anything as I walked beside her. It gave me a chance to think. The way Eve said, “It’s something else,” sounded like she wanted me to ask what made her quiet and sad. It’s what’s called an opening. Would my shyness let this opportunity slip through my fingers?

I thought about what I’d asked Adam on the bus. Eve’s story couldn’t be anything like that. Our laughing together at lunch had broken the ice. Did Adam’s sexy story make me bold? I decided to go for it. If Eve didn't feel like answering, I'd apologize and never ask anything personal again.

"If you're not shy," I said, "then what's the problem?"

"My parents just got a divorce."

"I'm sorry."

"Me, too. Maybe it was for the best. They fought half the time."

"In front of you?"

"Sometimes. Verbal battles. Always arguing over unimportant stuff."

"Sounds like me and my little brother."

"Yeah. They acted like kids. Being a grownup isn't the same as acting grownup."

"I guess not." I didn't know what to say next. I felt bad for Eve. I wondered what I'd do if my folks broke up and I had to move away from all my friends.

I couldn't stand the silence, so I asked, "Why did your mom move you here?"

"Couple of reasons. My grandparents, my mother's parents, live here. Mom trained at the local hospital and a job she qualified for suddenly opened up."

"I think you'll like it here. Do you enjoy sports?"

"Some. I'm not big on football, but I like to watch baseball and basketball games. Dad started to teach me golf. The sport I love best is swimming. I competed on a league team in Atlanta." That was promising. Some girls turn up their noses when they hear the word sports.

"I'm on a baseball team at the Boys' Club. You're welcome

to watch us play."

"Thanks. I'd like that. Are there any swimming teams around?"

"Sure. I know a girl at school who practices with our high school swim team. She can't take part in the meets, but it gets her ready for next year. I'll introduce you to her tomorrow."

"Thanks, Josh. You've been a big help. I'm glad I met you."

"Talking of practice, I'm gonna be late for mine."

"See you tomorrow," I heard Eve yell as I raced off.

No wonder Eve didn't run around with a big smile on her face. New town, new school, lost friends, those were bad enough. Toss in divorce and they added up to Hell. It gave me a stronger appreciation for my family as we gathered around the dining table to break bread that evening.

I felt so full of good will I didn't even tease Trav. My being so nice confused him. He looked at me suspiciously, thinking I'd planted a trap for him to fall into.

Dad trotted out his worst joke yet. "How many graduate students does it take to change a light bulb?"

Mom teaches graduate students, so he meant it for her. "I give up," she said without even trying. "How many graduate students does it take to change a light bulb?"

"Only one." Dad paused for effect. "But it takes them seven years to do it." He thought this was good stuff, but it flew past me like a fastball.

"Was that supposed to be funny?"

"Look, Joshua," Dad tried to explain. "Graduate students are famous for taking forever to finish their degrees. Haven't you heard them called gradual students?"

"No. I've got some homework. May I please be excused?"

I've never liked math, but eighth-grade algebra had me baffled. We were into graphing and, honestly, I've had more fun in a dentist's chair. I might've tried harder if I thought I'd ever use it, but my future plans don't run in a mathematical direction.

Let me be honest. I didn't have my whole mind tuned in to algebra. Other channels kept coming in, and some of them gave my math homework a run for its money.

The one getting the most airtime was the Adam and Marty show. Images of her naked body, or how I imagined it, kept popping up in inappropriate places. I'd be in the middle of plotting a point on the X, Y axis and there she'd be, smiling at me.

With math a lost cause, I tried reading my history assignment. No relief there. Reading about the Revolutionary War, I pictured myself sprawled on a battlefield, a bullet hole in my uniform and Marty beside me with a pail of cool water, mopping my fevered brow.

"Bed" kept creeping into my assigned essay for English, and that made me think of Marty in her underwear lying beside a boy. But the boy wasn't Adam. It was me.

I finally gave up on homework and crawled into my own empty bed. After the sexy stuff I'd imagined, it felt empty and lonely.

My sleep was restless, disturbed by dreams of Marty's long black hair flowing over her white female flesh, the subtle scent of perfume, her warm, soft body pressed to mine. My first wet dream came that night.

Chapter Five

My body's timing was on target since the school's sex education program got underway the next week. We heard words like puberty and hormones, helping us understand and deal with our sexually developing bodies.

The coaches ran separate classes for boys and girls. We could write down any questions with no names attached and get honest answers. The science teachers handled the technical stuff—sexual physiology they called it—the organic functioning and medical and health issues of the birds' and bees' business.

I learned that guys might have an erection every ninety minutes during sleep. When your testicles begin to produce semen, it can come out at night as mine did. It's a sign a boy's become a man just like menstruation signals a girl's become a woman.

"Here's sex in a nutshell," our science teacher said. "A sperm in the semen fertilizes the egg in a womb, the egg develops into a fetus, and a baby is born."

Maturing into a man I found both exciting and scary. The

power to create a human being brought with it tremendous responsibilities. The morning after my dream I studied myself in the bathroom mirror. I didn't look any different, or did I? Could I see the beginning of a mustache above my upper lip?

"Hi," I said to Eve at the bus stop. "Ready for another exciting school day?"

"Is there something special about today?"

"I'm joking. Classes have all excitement of watching paint dry."

Eve laughed. "At least paints are colorful. Schoolwork is gray. That paper we've got to write for English has me worried. I'd rather paint all day than write."

"It's not that bad. It's algebra that's awful."

"Are you kidding? Algebra's a breeze. Research writing's the bad news."

"You must think better in numbers than words."

"I always have. Numbers make more sense. They're clear, no double meanings, and the rules don't keep changing."

"English is a difficult language," I agreed. "But it's better than you make out. I love to write. It's fun to pick the right words out of thousands and then arrange them in different ways."

"I'm glad you like it," Eve said. "It's always been hard for me. And what's the point of diagramming sentences? It's a waste of time."

"I love diagramming. Think of it as a puzzle where you have to put each word in the right place."

"But what's the point?"

"It helps you understand how sentences work. Even if it didn't, it's still fun."

"For you. I've got better things to do."

"Like plotting little points on an axis?"

"Okay, so we have different tastes and talents. Can we agree to disagree?"

"Deal." I held out my hand and we shook on it. It was the first time we touched. Her fingers and palm were warm and I didn't want to let go.

Adam didn't ride the bus that morning, but he was already at school when we arrived. "Hey, Eve," he called. "Can I see you a minute?"

"Sure. What is it?"

Adam gave me a look that meant, "Get lost!"

I got the message. "See you two later," I said. "I've got to finish a few algebra problems before third period."

I didn't lie, but I also didn't do those problems. I tried to imagine what Adam might say to Eve that he didn't want me to hear. I figured it had to do with getting her as his girlfriend. But Eve had a first-class brain. She'd see through any line he tried to sell her. She was way above Amy Lynne and her friends that fell at Adam's feet.

Was I jealous? Maybe. I wanted to believe that a girl might like me more than him. But not any girl. We were competing for the same girl. Think of the Garden of Eden with three instead of two. One of us had to be the snake.

Eve and I were friends. We got along great. But I wanted to be more than her friend. I wanted us to be boyfriend and girlfriend. A couple. Going steady. I'd never had a relationship like that or wanted one. Why now? Was it this special girl or physical maturity? Probably all of the above.

I fantasized my way through class after class, picturing Eve and me holding hands as we went to the bus, maybe meeting to sneak a quick kiss between classes. Could my daydream come true? Boy, did I want to think so.

At lunch with Eve I was dying to know what Adam said to her, but I didn't think it polite to ask. I wanted her to tell me so I wouldn't look interested. It didn't work that way. She asked my how my algebra class went and wanted advice on a topic for her English paper.

With lunch almost over, I couldn't stand it any longer. I broke down and asked my nosy question. "What was Adam up to this morning?"

"Up to?" Eve frowned. Did she dislike my question or did it confuse her?

"You know, wanting to talk to you alone, like he had a secret to share."

"It wasn't secret. You could've stayed."

"That's not the message I got. You didn't see how Adam looked at me."

"It wasn't a big deal."

I was dying to shout, "So, what was it?" But I kept my mouth shut until I couldn't stand the suspense any longer.

"What did Adam say?"

"He apologized."

"Apologized?"

"Yeah. Said he was sorry about the gossip going around about us."

"Us?"

"Him and me. Remember? The story about me being his girlfriend."

"Oh. How did he explain it?"

"That he told some friends about me. Said I was pretty. That they put two and two together and came up with the idea on their own. He said some kids think he's girl crazy."

I bit my tongue to keep from saying, "He is." Eve would discover that on her own.

"He asked me to forget it and let him start over. Adam doesn't want me to be upset with him over nothing."

"That was it?"

"That was it. He's really sweet. Asked if we could be good friends."

"Just friends?"

"Yeah. Something wrong with that?"

"Of course not. He's a great guy. We've been friends and teammates since sixth grade."

"Good. Then let's all be friends, like the Three Musketeers."

"All for one and one for all." I hadn't read the book but I'd seen the movie.

"Adam asked me to come to your game Saturday. Are you okay with that?"

"Sure. You can be our special cheerleader."

That made Eve laugh. "The only cheer I know is *Two Bits*."

"That'll work." I remembered something from sixth-grade

social studies. "Why don't you present a scarf to the one of us who plays best? You know, like a medieval lady at a knight's jousting tournament."

"A little friendly competition? Sure, why not?"

"Why not indeed? Thank you fair damsel."

I was back to being a knight in shining armor again, ready to ride to Eve's rescue. Okay, Adam wasn't exactly a dragon, but he was competition. One thing I did know, come game day I'd play my damnedest.

I felt great about the way things were going. Eve and I were hitting it off. I'd never been with a girl like her and, the more I saw, the more I saw to like. With my head in the clouds, my feet fell flat to Earth in science class when I learned I'd become a daddy. Me? The father of a baby?

Before you think I sniffed some airplane glue, let me explain. Our teacher tried an experiment with our class. As part of our sex education lesson, we'd get to experience how it felt to be a parent.

She went around the room giving out babies, one to a customer. Of course they weren't living, breathing babies but only five-pound sacks of flour. We were to carry them around for a month and treat them as if they were real.

"If you take this seriously," she said, "you'll see what a big responsibility parenthood is. What will your babies require of you?"

Someone said, "Protection."

Another said, "Feed it."

"Good," she said. "What else?"

Two kids chimed in with, "Love it."

"Excellent. Babies need lots of love."

Adam held his nose and, with a squeaky voice, said, "Change its diapers."

That got a big laugh. When we quieted down, our teacher went on with the lesson.

"Being physically mature enough to create a baby doesn't mean you're ready for the many responsibilities it requires. This experience will help you discover that. Keep a journal of your feelings so we can discuss them at the end of the month."

I cradled my baby in my arms as we walked to our bus, but Adam put his in his backpack. "Like a papoose," he said.

I said, "We need names for them."

"Rose," he said. "I'm calling mine Rose."

"Why Rose?"

"Because a rose is a flower and this baby is filled with flour."

"You and your puns. If I wasn't named Josh, I'd like Scott for a name. I think I'll use it for my baby."

"So what are we going to do with these little bundles of joy at baseball practice today."

"You're right, Adam. And then there's our big game Saturday."

"One thing's for sure. I'm not letting this bag of flour spoil my fun."

"We'll need a sitter." Spotting Eve up ahead, I said, "I think I've found us one."

Eve graciously agreed to care for both babies that afternoon and during the next day's game.

"You're sure you know what to do?" I joked. "Two babies can be a handful."

"I had a childcare unit in home economics last year. I think I remember enough to get by."

"If you're lucky, they might take a nap."

"Should I give them a bath?"

"What? No! If you mix water and flour, we'll have a bag of paste. Dust them with a dry cloth when necessary."

"Only kidding. Go to your practice. Rose and Scott will be rested and ready when their daddies come for them."

After practice, Adam and I went to pick up our kids. I realized I had to think first of Scott and that I came second. I couldn't do whatever I wanted, whenever I wanted, wherever I wanted.

Eve had wrapped our babies in blankets, blue for mine and pink for Adam's. Rose even had a ribbon taped to the top of her head. Bundled up like that they almost passed for real babies.

"You guys want a soft drink?" Eve asked.

"You bet," Adam said. "Practice was hot and dusty."

Eve got three bottles from the fridge and put them on a tray with a bowl of ice and some glasses. I opened the sliding glass door for her and we walked over to a table and chairs on the pool deck.

Adam raised his glass and touched it to ours. "Here's to Josh," he toasted. "The boy who knocked the ball out of the park today. It had homerun written all over it."

"If I can just do it when it really counts, like Saturday's game."

"Scott would've been so proud of his daddy," Adam continued.

I panicked. "Scott! Where's Scott? I forgot all about him."

"You laid him on the kitchen counter when you helped me with the drinks." Eve found this funny. "I hoped he hasn't crawled over the edge and busted his head open."

It was Adam's time to panic. "I left Rose somewhere, too. Now I can't remember where."

"Great fathers you guys will make," Eve said. "You're likely to leave the baby at the gas station and remember it a hundred miles down the road."

"Give us a little time," I protested. "Parenthood takes getting used to."

"If they'd only cry a little," Adam added. "It'd help us remember them. These babies are too good."

"Not like you were, I'll bet," giving Adam a little jab. "You probably demanded so much attention your parents wished you were a bag of flour."

"I've heard my mom tell people I was a wonderful baby."

"Don't be so hard on Adam," Eve said, coming to his defense.

"You don't have him for a lab mate in science. He fools around half the time."

"Sounds like a fun lab," she said.

"It is, until we get our grades."

"Grades in middle school aren't important," he said. "They don't count until high school. I'll get serious then."

I shook my head in disbelief. "I'll believe it when I see it."

Adam got up, walked to the edge of the pool and splashed some water my way. "Boy," he said, "a swim sure would be refreshing. I'd strip off my uniform and dive in if I wasn't worried my manly muscles would turn Eve on."

"You wish."

"I'll jump in fully dressed," he said. "Somebody dare me."

"What would your mother say," Eve asked, "if you came to dinner sopping wet?"

"Probably wouldn't blink an eye," I offered. "To live with Adam is to expect the unexpected."

Suddenly serious, he looked at his watch. "Whoops! Gotta run. Dinner out tonight. Pizza! Yum yum."

Adam was well on his way when Eve called him back. "Aren't you forgetting something?"

"No. Like what?"

"Like Rose, your baby girl."

"Oh, yeah. Thanks," he shouted as he scooped her up and raced out the door.

Eve and I looked at each other and smiled. This baby business had its fun moments. "Penny for your thoughts," I said to break the silence.

"I was thinking about Adam. He's a little crazy, but in a good way. You never know what he'll do next. I think he would've jumped in the pool if I'd dared him."

"I'm surprised he didn't without your encouragement. That boy will do anything for a laugh."

"Is Adam ever serious?"

"Sometimes." I didn't add it usually involved a girl. I'll

admit I felt hurt. Eve's thoughts were for him and not me. The green-eyed jealousy monster was after me again, nipping at my heels.

"How long do you figure his sack of flour will last?"

"Without our help, not long."

"Then let's help him."

"Let's help each other."

"What do you mean?"

"I mean with our school work. I'll help you with your English paper, you help me with my algebra."

"Wow! Great idea."

"I get one now and then."

I didn't confess that this great idea got me one-on-one time with Eve. If Adam still won her heart, I'd at least end up with a better grade in algebra.

"Baseball season ends this week. Saturday's championship game wraps things up. Want to start after that?"

"Sure."

"Where'll we meet?"

"How about here? I'll ask my mom if we can be study partners."

With perfect timing, Ms. Williams came in from work. I introduced her to Scott.

"What a handsome baby," she said. "He must take after his mother because he doesn't look a thing like you."

I liked her sense of humor. Some parents lose their funny bones as they grow older. Eve's mom was different. So was my dad, even if his jokes fell flat. She also gave us permission to study together.

I felt great—private time with Eve and help with my worst class. If I could outplay Adam in the big game and win her scarf, I'd have a triple play. He might be better at baseball and getting girls than me, but I'd give him stiff competition, on and off the field. The time had come to play hardball.

Chapter Six

The day of the championship game couldn't have been more perfect. Seventy degrees, a sky bluer than blue, the grass so green the white lines of the diamond seemed etched on an emerald, what more might I want?

That's easy. I wanted my team to win; I wanted to outplay Adam; and I wanted to win Eve's scarf as well as her affection. It was a big day and I meant to claim it.

Excited, I woke early, put on my spotless uniform, and was first on the field. As members of the opposing team arrived, they joked how they'd cream us, but I stayed cool as a glass of iced tea. I had such confidence in our win a strong wind couldn't shake it. I would've bet my baseball card collection on it, including my mint condition, rookie Nolan Ryan.

I felt like a three-year-old thoroughbred in the starting gate, feeling my oats and ready to run. Not that horse racing's like baseball, except both are sports. Our game requires teamwork. One player can't carry it all.

Their coach called as the umpire flipped a quarter into the air. I tried to believe if we won the toss we'd win the game. We lost. So much for optimism. "Tails," the ump yelled. "Wildcats on the field. Panthers at bat. Play ball!"

Play ball? Not yet. I couldn't see Eve. I'd been scanning the bleachers but the more I looked, the more she wasn't there. Did she forget? She said she liked baseball, knew this game decided the championship for our league. Even more, it was a tournament between Adam and me. A trial of skill for the love of a lady. Okay, for her scarf.

I really panicked big league when I couldn't see Adam. Where in the Devil's hotspot was that goof-off? Looking for Eve caused me to forget him. I figured he had to be in the crowd before the two teams separated to play. But he wasn't. Did Adam's absence as well as Eve's mean something? Were they together? My heart raced.

Jealousy sucks. You imagine the worst. But that's how I felt about Eve and Adam. Could they both be no-shows at the same time? Didn't seem likely. What was up?

Then I heard our coach yell, "Adam, get your butt on second base."

I looked in that direction. There was Adam, pushing his bike, in no rush, like he had all the time in the world and then some. I don't think he even heard the coach, oblivious to everything but Eve walking beside him.

I swear smoke started from the coach's ears. His face turned red as his blood pressure soared into the danger zone. Still, Adam only had eyes for Eve.

She's the one who heard the coach's call. She also had sense to see the game was ready to start. Whatever she said, Adam dropped the bike where he stood and rushed toward the field.

"Nice of you to join us, Adam." I had to give him some grief. "Hope this early hour didn't put you out too much."

If he caught my sarcasm, it didn't show. "Sorry, Josh, old boy. Time got away from me."

How could he look at both his watch and Eve? Time's the last thing he had on his mind, and I didn't need three guesses to know what the first thing was. I had the same thing on the front burner of my brain.

"I've decided to hit a four-bagger every time I'm at the plate," Adam called as he raced past me. "That should impress Eve."

I knew Adam well enough to read his face, and the face I read did not have baseball front and center. I'd bet his thoughts were still on Eve. Did he hear the crack of a bat on a fastball?

The ball hit the ground, rolling at me like a live grenade. I turned, dropped to one knee, scooped it into my glove, and threw automatically to Adam on second base as I saw the batter round first and keep running.

"Adam," I yelled. "Wake up!"

He snapped to attention. Only his quick reflexes enabled him to catch the ball in time, slicing it thin. A closer shave would've drawn blood.

Adam's lack of concentration could've easily given our opponents a homerun. It was serious enough for the coach to stroll out for a little chat with his second baseman. All right, chat's the wrong word since the coach did all the talking. Talking's the wrong word, too. Shouting describes it better.

The coach's arms were rotating like windmills as he got in Adam's face. I couldn't hear all of it, but the message came through loud and clear, though not as polite as I'm reporting it—Get your eye on the ball and your mind on the game or I'll kick you off the field and the team simultaneously.

Our coach is no intellectual giant, and his language can be profane, but he *is* proficient at pitching his point across the plate. What he said and how he said it focused Adam's attention on nothing but baseball. For the rest of the game he didn't even look Eve's way as she cheered us on from the bleachers.

Adam respects a superior force, and our coach is nothing if not that. A superior force also summed up our opponents. The Panthers lived up to their name in every way, and I couldn't help thinking, as wild as wildcats are, they're no match for a full-grown panther.

They ran roughshod over us and used a bat like a six-shooter, sending a spray of hits into every corner of the field. It took our best efforts to keep them to three runs the first half inning. The Panthers came to win, and there seemed no way to stop them. But I'd come to win myself, at least Eve's scarf if not the game. That's what I determined as we abandoned the diamond for the dugout.

Adam had stopped their streak with a sick catch of a fly ball, giving them three outs and bringing our fans to their feet. He gave a little bow, grinning, pleased with his performance. He probably thought that put him ahead in our personal competition, which it did, but for only a moment. What it did do was top off the tank of my fury, fueled by Adam's arrival with Eve.

It's not good to get angry in sports, 'cause you lose control and can't play your best. Picture my mind right then as a wasp's nest struck hard with a stick. Those little stingers were aching to jab Adam's ass.

It's hard to maintain outer control when inside your temper's boiling. My guts were twisted tighter than a rubber band on a balsa wood airplane. When I let it go, all hell would break loose.

And it did. Not hell, but the baseball. I was leadoff man in the lineup, and I came to the plate at fever pitch. I gripped the bat, swinging hard as the pitcher fired the pill from the hill, my eyes shut tight. Blind luck connected bat to ball, hitting it high and far, farther than I'd ever done before.

I dropped the bat and ran, not looking left or right or pausing on the bases. From that sound of wood on leather, I sensed the ball soaring over the outfielders. My instincts shouted, "Homerun!"

They said right. I reached second base before the ball was recovered, rounded third and hit the home stretch when the second baseman got it, sliding to the plate seconds before the ball reached the catcher's mitt.

If the fans cheered me on, I didn't hear them. During my race around the bases my brain blocked out everything but running and breathing. My teammates rushed to surround me, slapping my backside and yelling like crazy. It was only then I realized what I'd done. I owed it all to my anger at Adam, but I knew better than to try it again.

The congratulations were great. I won't deny it. Yet, what really mattered to me was what Eve thought, and I wouldn't learn that till the game ended.

In the dugout I looked for Adam's reaction. He congratulated me on a fine play, and I knew he was happy about our side's first run. But what about the other game going on, the one between him and me?

My homerun put him behind. He'd made that tremendous catch in the first inning, and now I had him eating my dust. I will say this for Adam, if he had hard feelings, he didn't let on. With his self-confidence, he probably figured he'd surpass me later.

I believe it was then that Adam understood the contest for Eve's scarf was, for me, more than a game. Did he sense my determination to win? No words were exchanged, but he had to feel the purpose and power within me.

For Adam it was more of a lark. Eve was one out of many where he was concerned. Plenty of girls got goggle-eyed over him, but he certainly saw her as a challenge. She didn't bow before him or beg for his attention.

For me it was different. Eve had something special and I wanted to be special to her. Don't laugh, but I saw baseball as the battlefield where I might win her.

Even if he didn't feel as strongly about Eve as I did, Adam was a fighter. He'd outdo my homerun or die trying. When he finally got to bat, we had two outs and only one run, mine. Two of our guys were on base, one on first and one on third. All we needed was another homerun to put us in the lead, and that's exactly what Adam attempted. Trouble was, he tried too hard.

Fortune, luck, whatever you call it, smiled on me when I belted the ball with my eyes closed. It frowned on Adam. He put great power into his swings, only to connect with air.

Two runs behind, we trusted Adam's skill and strength to give us the lead, and that included me. No way I'd bet against our team. But the guys didn't blame him. They knew he was a great player. He'd tried. Given all the energy in him. Even the best strike out. Ask Babe Ruth if you don't believe it.

The following innings were uneventful. Neither side played with superstar power. The final inning found our team three runs behind. Outplayed is a nice way to put it.

The final inning brought a sad bunch of Wildcats to home plate. Two quick outs did nothing to raise our spirits. A fumbled catch took me to first base and the two guys after me got a single apiece. Was our bad luck evaporating or were we finally playing like we should've from the start? Whatever, the bases were loaded.

That was the picture when Adam stepped up to bat. He might be a showoff and joker half the time, but the boy took baseball seriously. His face frozen in concentration, he didn't smile or make his usual tip of the hat to the pitcher, but shouldered that bat like a gun.

The guy up after Adam happened to be our weakest batter. His record for striking out in this game was perfect, and no one figured he'd do any better. That meant nothing but a grand slammer would do. Anything less and we lost. All eyes focused on Adam.

Till then I'd outplayed him. If a homerun escaped my competitor, I'd win Eve's scarf. But the Wildcats must lose for me get it. "No way," I said to myself. "I'd die before I ever wished that." Then I joined my teammates cheering Adam on.

The first pitch was a curve ball Adam missed by five miles. Must've been nervous, 'cause he seldom swung wild. He took a deep breath, glaring at the pitcher, ready for whatever came next.

It was a fastball and a second strike. You could feel the tension in our team and even in the stands. Like we'd all turned to stone, expectant for fate's decree.

Did I see "DETERMINATION" tattooed on Adam's arm? He'd never shown such concentration. The pitcher looked left and right, then, without a pause, put the ball right over home plate.

KERWHOP! The bat hit the ball like an explosion, sending it up in a rainbow's arch to the farthest corner of the field, far beyond the outermost outfielder. Our trio of boys raced home with Adam hot on their heels. The Wildcats had won!

We mobbed him, lifting our savior to our shoulders. Someone poured a bottle of Gatorade over the coach's head. We hugged and ran around like wild men, unbelievably happy. Our dream came true. We were the champions.

While my team won, I lost. I scanned the bleachers for Eve and saw her standing among the fans, going crazy with cheering, but the cheers were for Adam and not for me.

The excitement settled down and players and fans wandered away until only Eve, Adam, and I remained. Slowly, she removed the scarf from her neck, presenting it to Adam. "Hail the conquering hero," she said, half seriously, half humorously.

"Thank you, my lady," he replied with a bow. "I shall forever cherish this gift you so kindly bestow." Then he kissed her on the cheek, executing a wheelie on his bike as he sped away.

Adam deserved Eve's scarf. No one could argue otherwise. Still, I couldn't help wishing she'd presented it to me.

An embarrassed silence settled between us. Finally, I said, "Adam walked you to the game. I figured he'd see you home."

"His grandfather's ill. They're packed and ready to leave, waiting for the game to be over."

"Oh. I see."

"You can walk me home if you'd like."

"I'd like that very much, my lady," I replied, echoing Adam.

In keeping with our medieval play, I offered her my hand. Eve accepted and, linking arm in arm, we strolled toward home, reliving the day's momentous events.

"Where's Scott today?" she suddenly asked.

"My mom's got him. I promised to clean out the garage if she'd play babysitter. I wonder what Adam did with Rose."

"Put her in round-the-clock daycare is my guess."

I laughed. "Sounds exactly like him."

When we reached her house, Eve opened her purse, pulling out another scarf. I shook my head as if to refuse, but she stopped me. "Adam may have ended the game with his homerun, but you began it with yours. You each played like pros."

Then, as Adam had done to her, Eve leaned over and kissed me on the cheek. She was through the front door before I could thank her. It was the happiest day of my life.

Raising my fingers to my face, I touched the spot still warm from her lips. Then I laid those fingers on my lips, trying to transfer the feel of her kiss. It felt like my insides were melting.

Could life get any better? No, not if I batted a thousand. I held Eve's scarf, sweet with the scent of perfume, to my face.

"Love," I whispered. "I'm in love."

Chapter Seven

Monday morning I sprang from bed earlier than usual. The excitements of Saturday, winning the championship, Eve's gift of a scarf, not to mention a kiss, were still bubbling in my blood. I sensed a great adventure opening before me, an adventure changing my life forever.

I felt as though braced at the open door of an airplane, a parachute strapped to my back, looking down at a world far below. I wanted to make the jump, free falling into a wild, wonderfully foreign place. No way I'd stay safely on the plane, returning to the runway where I'd started.

Ahead of schedule, I suddenly decided to stop at Eve's house and walk with her to the bus stop. I pictured the surprised but pleased smile on her face. I hoped that she hoped I'd come for her.

Eve's mom must've been standing by the door, 'cause it opened the moment I knocked. She startled me so I couldn't remember what I'd come for.

"Good morning, Joshua." She smiled as she looked at my bag of flour wrapped in a baby blanket. "How's Scott today?"

"He's fine," I stammered, shifting him from one arm to the other. "Is Eve here?"

"She left five minutes ago."

"Oh. I was gonna walk her to the bus."

"I'm afraid Adam beat you to it."

"Adam!" I exclaimed before I could collect myself. What was up with him? He never gets anywhere on time and suddenly he's ten minutes early on a Monday morning.

"Thanks, Ms. Williams. I'll see them at our stop. Sorry to bother you."

"No bother, Joshua. Can you explain why Adam had a scarf of Eve's tied to the back of his baseball cap?"

I couldn't believe it. The jerk was gonna walk around school with Eve's scarf hanging down his neck like the raccoon tail on Davy Crockett's hat. He'd probably start a new fad like he did in sixth grade when he wore board shorts and half the boys followed suit. Adam did have style, I'll admit that much, but I'd pass on following his lead. A copycat I'm not.

I reached in my right pocket and felt the scarf Eve gave me. It was smooth and silky like I remembered her lips on my cheek. Blood flooded my face as I blushed.

What did Ms. Williams ask me? She waited for an answer while I tried to remember. Oh, yes, Adam's hat and Eve's scarf.

"He won it."

She gave me a look like the grits weren't in the middle of my plate.

"In the baseball game, I mean. We, Adam and me, had a contest. Eve promised a scarf to the one who played best. You know, like knights in the Middle Ages."

It suddenly sounded silly, even to me. Kid stuff really. But she seemed to understand. Maybe she'd done something similar as a girl.

"Of course." She nodded. "Improve performance with a prize."

"Something like that." There was more to it than winning a baseball game, but she could see that herself. Why two boys knocked on your door the same morning, wanting to walk your daughter to school, wasn't a mystery requiring Sherlock Holmes' special skills.

I looked at my watch. "Sorry, gotta run."

"Have a great day, Joshua."

I was anxious to see what was up between Adam and Eve before we boarded the bus. I saw the whole gang gathered around Adam as he recounted his championship-winning homerun, making a great story even greater. He's so entertaining and adds so much color to his tales you forgive the fact that some of it skirts the truth. He'd convince you he won the game single handedly.

Whatever line he was feeding them must've been funny, 'cause they were all laughing. I heard Eve's wonderful laugh above the others. It wasn't polite to break into Adam's yarn, but I did.

"What's so funny? Did the school burn down?"

Adam chuckled. "I wish."

"What, then?" I looked at Eve.

"Adam's telling us about the players on your ball team. He

makes them sound so funny, but I think he exaggerates a little."

"More than a little, I'd guess."

"Probably. He said the team's done much better since the pitcher got his curve ball straightened out. Where does he get this stuff?"

I could've said he got that line from Joe Garagiola, but I didn't. Let Adam have the spotlight. I could've also warned Eve about his come-on lines with girls, but I figured she'd spot them herself.

Adam stuck close to Eve as we got on the bus and, when Eve slid onto a window seat, he sat beside her. I took a seat several rows back, close enough to see but not to hear them. He did all the talking, as usual, and made her laugh. I hoped I wasn't one of the players he made fun of.

Knowing Adam as I did, most of the stories involved him. He enjoyed making himself the butt of his humor as often as he picked on others. An equal opportunity joker, everything and everyone were fair game. If only I could make Eve laugh like he did.

My morning classes were dull, as usual, but I got by thinking of lunch with Eve. She'd started bringing her lunch, so we headed for our usual spot in the corner.

I meant to ignore Adam entirely, meaning his performance off and on the bus that morning. And I tried. I really did. But I couldn't. His monopolizing Eve got to me. I knew the more I mentioned his name, the more important it made him, but I seemed powerless to stop.

"Adam was on center stage this morning," I commented,

hoping Eve would tell me everything he'd said. No such luck. She didn't.

"He's on center stage all day long," she said.

That's all she'd give me, something I'd known for years. Adam had a plan in mind, and he was proceeding carefully. I'd seen him work his magic with girls before, but then I had no interest in the girls he worked it on. Now I did.

I kept quiet. If Eve wanted to talk to me about Adam, she'd have to do it on her own. I gave up trying to make it happen.

"He's a crazy guy," she said after five minutes of silence. "Where does his energy come from?"

"Adam's like the Energizer Bunny. His batteries keep going and going and going."

Eve had a question about her English paper that I steered back to our mutual friend. "You could do what Adam does," I said.

"What's that?"

"Let the computer write your paper."

"I didn't know it could."

"Sure. Just Google your topic, go to ten or more sites, find stuff that sounds good, copy and paste it, change the order of the words and add some words of your own, make some grammatical and spelling mistakes, and there you are."

"Sounds too easy."

"It works for Adam 'cause his teachers don't expect much from him. They're amazed he even turns in an assignment, so they give him a 'C' and everyone's happy."

"I think I'll stick with the old-fashioned way."

"You mean write it yourself?"

"Yes, but I still want your help."

"You've got it. And I still need your assistance with algebra."

"Of course."

Eve looked puzzled.

"What is it?" I asked.

"Adam's not dumb. So why doesn't he take schoolwork seriously?"

"You've heard him. He's waiting till high school when it really counts. He sees middle school as the last chance for fun."

"He's good at it."

"None better."

"Adam talked about the school dance Friday night. Are you going?"

"I dunno. Hadn't thought about it. Are you?"

"Adam asked me to go with him."

So that was his game plan. He knew I never went to dances. Eve would be his alone. I had to ask, "So, are you going?"

"Sure. Sounds like fun."

Yeah, for them, but not for me. "You'll have a good time. I've heard girls say Adam's a great dancer."

"How about you, Josh?"

"My dancing's okay, if the girl wears combat boots."

"I didn't mean your dancing. Are you coming to the dance?"

"Thanks, but I'd only be in the way."

"Whose way?"

"Yours and Adam's."

"But I'm not going with him."

"You're not?"

"No."

"I thought you said he asked you."

"He did."

"You turned him down?"

"Not exactly. I said I'd like to go, but not on a date. I want to be free to dance with any boy I like."

"Like me?"

"Yes, you, Adam, and other boys, too. On a date you're tied down. The boy always acts like you belong to him. If you look sideways at someone else, he gets jealous."

"That's normal, isn't it?"

"I guess. But I'm not ready for that kinda commitment. Maybe someday."

"That's how I feel," I said. But I didn't. I'd go steady in a heartbeat if Eve was the girl. I wanted to tell her how I felt and might've if my shyness hadn't stopped me. Probably better I didn't. I wouldn't apply any pressure like Adam would. Better to wait for the right time, if there ever was a right time. At least she'd turned Adam down, so I still had a chance.

"So, will you come?"

"If you insist." I smiled at the thought of me trying to dance. "But a slow dance is the best you'll get from me. And don't forget those boots."

Eve laughed and, picturing her dancing in combat boots, made me laugh, too.

"And who knows," I added, "a glamorous girl might fall in love with me at first sight."

"And a handsome prince might ride into the gym on a white horse, sweep me up, and take me for Whoppers and fries at Burger King."

"My glamour gal and I'll meet you there. Save us a booth and we'll double date."

We both found that thought funny. I loved that I could make Eve laugh, just like Adam did. Then the bell rang and I raced off to the locker room where I found him dressing in as I dressed out.

I decided to have a little fun with him, like he always does to me. "Eve asked me to go to the dance."

That stunned him, like a sock in the jaw. I'd never seen Adam at a loss for words. When his brain cleared, he said, "I asked her first. She said she didn't want a date but would dance with me."

"She told me the same thing."

"But you said she asked you to go."

"She did. But with the same conditions she gave you. Doesn't want to be tied to just one guy."

"We'll see about that. I think she'll change her mind before the party's over. Get your dance in early, Josh, 'cause I have an idea Eve will be leaving with me."

"What makes you so sure of that? One dance with me and she'll forget you even exist."

Adam laughed like a hyena at a comedy club. "Let me tell you something buddy boy. I've wrapped more than one girl around my little finger. Eve's playing hard to get now, but just you wait. No girl born can resist me for long."

What an ego! And confidence. I'd pay plenty for a pound of that. Did I lack faith in my masculine charms? Yeah, a little. Did shyness hold me back? Sure. I wondered what might happen if I let myself go? Could I use the dance to find out?

Honestly, I didn't know what my charms were, assuming I had any or, if I did, how to use them. I'd never cared enough about one girl to try. Until Eve.

I decided to give it a go. Work up the courage. If I sat out the dance and did nothing, Adam would have a clear field. I decided to make my move that Friday night—if I could figure one out.

I did try, but nothing seemed right. Eve sounded serious about not wanting to get serious. I'd respect that. If *I* seemed too serious it might ruin our developing friendship.

I finally decided to just relax and be myself. Being a fake led nowhere. I hoped Eve would see how much I cared for *her* and, if or when she felt the same toward me, I felt sure *I'd* see it. At least I hoped so.

It wasn't Adam's direct approach. It certainly wasn't a caveman's approach. You might not call it an approach at all. Yet, I had a hunch it might be the way to win her. If Eve could be won. This girl knew her own mind and called her own shots.

Adam's dad volunteered to drive us to the dance. We invited Eve to ride with us, but she had something to do with her mom first and said she'd meet us there. So, Adam and I showed up stag and waited for her to arrive.

"I'll flip you for the first dance with her," my baseball buddy suggested. "Heads I win. Tails you lose."

"You couldn't fool a first grader with that old trick," I said, shaking my head.

"Can't blame a guy for trying."

"More like cheating. We'll use my quarter. You probably picked up a trick coin at the magic shop."

"I'm your friend. Trust me."

"That's what Brutus said to Julius Caesar before he stabbed him."

"Have it your way. I always win coin tosses."

"May the best man win," I said, flipping the two-bit piece into the air.

Adam's famous luck didn't desert him. He called tails and tails it was. But I wasn't about to let him monopolize Eve. I'd cut in halfway through the first number.

When Eve walked in, all heads turned. And with good reason. She was dressed for an end-of-year prom, not a first-of-the-year gymnasium dance. The boys were all captivated and the girls jealous. The lady was drop-dead gorgeous.

Adam wasted no time sweeping her into his arms and dancing away from me. It came as a shock when I tapped him on the shoulder, cutting in halfway through the number. I don't think he'd seen me as competition until then. From the look on his face, happy he was not.

Naturally he cut in on me during the second dance. We traded Eve between us for the rest of the night. None of the other boys dared ask her to dance, sensing she was ours. If this bothered her, it didn't show. When she wanted to, Eve could conceal her feelings better than anyone.

"You sold yourself short, Josh," she said during a break. "Your footwork is wonderful."

"You'll change your opinion after I squash your feet. Do you have steel toes in your dancing slippers?"

"No. My mom took me to every shoe store in town and they were all sold out. I guess the girls heard you were coming to this dance and beat me to them."

I noticed Adam's face when Eve complimented my dancing. He has a high opinion of his moves on the dance floor and must've felt hurt when she didn't toss a compliment his way. His dancing is showy, putting all the attention on him and not his partner. But that's the way with everything Adam does.

I stayed focused on Eve. The slow dances were best, my body pressed against hers, her head on my shoulder with that silky hair caressing my face, the warmth of the bare flesh of her back beneath my hand.

I wanted desperately to kiss her cheek, cover her with kisses. We were so close it hurt. Couldn't she read my mind? I cursed my shyness.

After trading Eve back and forth through a half dozen dances, the three of us took a breather and made a beeline for the punch bowl. The sickly sweet drink passing as punch could only have been made by one of the slop slinger's in the cafeteria kitchen. The stuff was vile, but cold, and my body needed cooling down.

We went back to dancing and, when Adam cut in, I used the opportunity to visit the men's room. On returning, they'd disappeared. "That snake," I said to myself. "Just like him to whisk Eve away while my back is turned."

They couldn't of gone far. Once you leave a school dance, you're not allowed back. So, I started searching the gym's dark corners where couples try and make out before the roaming chaperones discover them.

I found the pair in an unexpected spot. The coach must've forgotten to lock the weight room door, a slip-up Adam used to his advantage. He probably got Eve in there on the pretext of showing her how many pounds he could bench press. I caught him accomplishing his real mission as I quietly opened the door.

What I saw sank my hopes like a torpedoed ship—Adam's arms wrapped tightly around Eve—his lips planted firmly on hers.

Chapter Eight

In my thirteen years I've seen enough films to know a kiss when I see one, and what they were doing was definitely a kiss. As a judge would say, it was beyond and to the exclusion of any reasonable doubt. Silently, I closed the door and slipped back onto the dance floor.

My feelings bounced from stunned, angry, jealous, to Elvis singing, "I'm all shook up." Shocked, knocked off my feet, paralyzed even. I wasn't sure where I was or what the hell was going on.

I left the gym to get some fresh air. Knowing I couldn't get back in, I called my dad to pick me up.

"How was the dance, Joshua?"

"Okay."

"Didn't you say Adam's dad was driving you home?"

"Yeah."

"So, what happened?"

"I had enough, that's all."

Dad's a clever guy, despite his light bulb jokes. He saw something was wrong. He also understood I didn't want to talk about it. So he turned up the satellite radio and hummed along while I brooded.

That weekend I stayed close to home. My mood was blue and I didn't want to accidentally run into Adam or Eve. I even hated the way their names sounded together.

If I hadn't seen them kissing, things would've been the same. Ignorance can be bliss. But I had seen, so things would never be the same again.

I had to face facts. Adam won Eve fair and square. I needed to back off and settle for Eve's friendship, but could I erase my romantic feelings? As long as my love for Eve lasted, I couldn't pretend life was merry in Happy Valley.

Mom was the first to notice my dragging ass attitude. She's always read me like a book, but this time she was on the wrong page.

"Aren't you feeling well, Joshua?"

"I'm fine."

"You don't look like someone who's feeling fine. There's a flu bug on the loose. Let me take your temperature."

"Mom, please! I'm a big boy now. I'll let you know if and when I feel sick."

By Sunday afternoon even Dad noticed I wasn't my usual cheery self. I'd fended off Mom's concern, but I couldn't escape his trial attorney questioning.

"How many psychiatrists does it take to change a light bulb?"

"Another time, Dad. I'm not in the mood."

"I'd say a little humor is the perfect prescription when life lets the air out of your tires."

"It'll take more than a light bulb joke to brighten me up." I smiled. "No pun intended."

"You see, I haven't even told my joke and you're feeling better already. Level with your old man. What's up? You haven't looked this miserable since you struck out every time at bat five games running."

"This is different."

"So, what is it? Trouble at school?"

"Kinda." I thought of the dance and the feel of Eve in my arms. Then I pictured her with Adam and their suck-face scene. The feeling of loss was a dull dagger in my heart.

"Look, Joshua. We've always been open with each other. There's nothing you can't tell me or ask me. Or you're free to say, 'Butt out.'"

"What can you tell me about girls?"

"Girls?"

"You know, the female of the species, the curvaceous ones."

He gave me a serious smile. "I'm no expert, but I'll try to help. What exactly do you want to know?"

"A little bit of everything. Like, what makes them tick? Why do they tell you they don't want to get involved with only one guy, and then they're gluing their lips to your friend?"

"Whoa! Did you just jump from girls as a gender to one girl in particular?"

"Okay, I'll confess. I'm in love."

"Any girl I know?"

"Eve, the new girl Mom tried to match me up with. I

started out liking her, and now I *really* like her."

"I see."

"What does being in love feel like? Mom thinks I have the flu, and I do sorta ache all over and feel feverish. But I'm not sick. I've never felt quite like this."

"That sounds normal enough. When you have it really bad, you walk into walls and can't get her out of your mind. Love sometimes feels so good it hurts."

"I'm tired of hurting. How do I make it stop?"

"Why do you want it to?"

"I wouldn't if Eve liked me like I like her."

"How do you know what her feelings are? Did she tell you?"

"Not in so many words. It's more what I saw than what she said."

"What did you see?"

"Eve and Adam kissing. At the dance. In the weight room where they thought nobody would see."

"I get the picture."

"She wouldn't have done that if she really cared about me, would she?"

"There may be more to it than meets the eye. Looks can be deceiving and eyewitnesses unreliable. I've seen that often during courtroom trials."

"I thought a picture was worth a thousand words."

"If the picture is accurate. Cameras can lie. Ask any movie star."

"I'm afraid to ask Eve. Afraid what I'd find out. Besides, she'd think I was snooping."

"Does Eve act as if she likes Adam? I mean romantically."

"No, that's the funny thing. Nothing adds up. She told both of us before the dance she didn't want to go steady with any one boy."

"That's promising."

"Maybe she changed her mind. Women are supposed to be famous for that, aren't they?"

"About like men, I'd say. No better, no worse."

"For real?"

"For real. There are many myths about women, but they are human. They're not so different from men. I'd say they're less afraid to express their feelings. Girls aren't raised to hide their emotions like boys are."

"Eve is open and honest. That's what puzzles me. If she really liked Adam, I think she'd say so. I know she enjoys his company 'cause he makes her laugh, but I'd swear she wasn't in love with him."

"There you are then. Go with your gut reaction. Talk to her. Let her know how you feel. I'll let you in on one fact about women."

"What's that?"

"They like men who will share their feelings with them. Women enjoy talking about things that make most men clam up. Try it and see."

"Thanks, Dad. I might do that if the right time comes along. I'm trying to get over some of my shyness, but it's hard."

"If you love her, you'll find a way."

He started to leave when I called him back. "Hey, Dad?"

"Yes?"

"How many psychiatrists does it take to change a light bulb?"

His face lit up. "It only takes one, but the light bulb has to really want to be changed." I heard him chuckling as he left the room.

He'd given me plenty to think about. Maybe my situation wasn't hopeless. But I'd have to go face-to-face with Eve to find out. Did I have the courage, and what if the truth wasn't what I wanted to hear?

The talk with Dad inspired me to explore the subject of women more deeply. This time I went straight to the source. I found her in the study reading essays she'd assigned her students.

"Mom?"

She laid down what she was reading and looked up.

"You're a woman, right?"

"The last time I looked."

"What I mean is, being a woman, you've also been a girl."

"It's difficult to get around that."

"Can we talk?"

"Always. About what?"

"Dad and I just had a man-to-man. Now I'd like a woman's advice."

"What's the subject?"

"Love."

"Ah! You've come to an expert. Not only am I a woman, but a woman who wrote her Ph.D. dissertation on the love sonnets of Elizabeth Barrett Browning."

"I didn't know that."

"It's not something that pops up in casual conversation. At least not outside a university English department."

"As an expert, what does a girl feel like when she's in love?"

"How does a boy feel?"

"I asked you first."

"That was a rhetorical question. The kind that doesn't require an answer. My point is that love is love. Being male or female doesn't much matter. The feeling is universal."

"Maybe I asked the wrong question. What I'm really after is how to tell if a girl's in love? If they feel the same as boy's inside, do they act differently on the outside?"

"Joshua, tell me to mind my own business, but is this interest in love personal or academic?"

"A bit of both. Adam says the new girl, Eve, is in love with him, but I don't see any signs of it."

"Is he in love with her?"

"I dunno. You know Adam. If a girl's got the goods, he's in love with her."

"More like lust, I imagine. There's a big difference, though it's often difficult separating them."

"I suppose."

Dad and I hadn't discussed lust, another word for sex, but since Mom brought it up, I plunged ahead. These talks could be a good exercise in overcoming my shyness.

"Adam's not the only person in the picture. I'm trying to paint myself into it, too."

"You like Eve. Adam likes Eve. Does Eve like you or Adam? Is that what it comes to?"

"You nailed it."

"In my experience, if a girl likes a boy or, even more, loves him, she'll let him know."

"What if a boy likes a girl and she doesn't like him?"

"Happens all the time. And vice versa. Unrequited love is when the one you love doesn't love you in return. The ancient Romans believed there was a special place in Hades, we'd say Hell, reserved for unrequited lovers."

"That bad, huh?"

"Can be. If you let it. Remember, there's more that one fish in the sea."

"You lost me."

"Look around. There are other girls in your middle school."

"Thanks, Mom, but there's only one I want to hook."

"I understand. Remember, Joshua, I'm here anytime you need a listener."

The talks with my folks helped but didn't extinguish the flames I felt burning inside me. Sure, there were other girls, but right then I wanted no one but Eve. I wasn't about to give in to Adam. Not yet. There was plenty of fight left in me.

Monday morning I deliberately missed the bus by hanging around the house till it was too late. Dad had to drop me off on his way to the courthouse. I felt bad slowing him down, but no way was I ready to see Adam sitting beside Eve all the way to school.

I hadn't seen or heard from either one since the dance

Friday night. I knew the longer I put it off the harder it'd be to meet up with them again. I was uncertain what to say, how to act, or how to react. Would their feelings for each other be observable, or would they try to hide what happened in that weight room?

I knew I couldn't avoid Eve at lunch. If I didn't appear at our table, as usual, she'd wonder what was up. I arrived first, opened my lunch bag, put on my everything's okay face, and waited.

I didn't know what to expect. I thought I might read something about Adam in her expression, but she looked the same. I readied myself for her first question.

"What happened to you at the dance? One minute you were there and the next you'd disappeared."

"Would you believe I suddenly remembered I had homework to do?"

"No, I would not."

"Didn't think so. What happened, I got a bad headache and called my dad to pick me up."

"I'm sorry. It was a fun dance."

Sure, I thought. For you! If you're idea of fun is smooching with a good-looking guy in the weight room.

"I tried to let you know I was leaving, but I couldn't find you." I paused. "Or Adam, either."

Did she blush? I wasn't certain, but I'd bet a week's allowance on it. Eve quickly changed the subject.

We didn't have much to say the rest of the lunch period. A chasm had opened between us, so wide we couldn't talk across it. Sometimes Eve's mouth would start to open, then it'd close before a word slipped through.

What could I say? If I admitted to spying on her and Adam, she'd probably get mad and never eat lunch with me again. I decided to keep my lips zipped.

As we went to toss our trash, Eve hesitated, then said, "Josh, your baseball practice is over now, right?"

"Right."

"So, do you still want to study together like we planned?"

"Do you?"

"Sure. Why not?"

"I thought since Friday you might've changed your mind."

"Why? What happened Friday?"

"Well, won't Adam mind if I start hanging out at your house?"

"What's he got to do with it? He doesn't have any say in who I invite over."

"He won't be jealous then?"

"Josh, spit it out. I'm not a mind reader."

"Shall I level with you?"

"Please."

"It's like this. I didn't mean to see what I saw but, since I did, I'll admit it."

"You lost me on the first curve. Double back for another try."

"I saw what happened between you and Adam at the dance."

"You did?"

"It wasn't snooping. I was looking for you."

"Are you talking about what happened in the weight room?"

"Yep."

"And what you saw makes you think Adam and I are an item?"

"Looked like it to me."

"What exactly did you see?"

"You and Adam kissing."

"That's all?"

"Isn't that enough?"

"Hardly. There was more."

"More!"

"Yes sir, much more. You should've watched a little longer."

"Why?"

"'Cause you'd of seen me slap the you-know-what out of your pal, Adam."

Chapter Nine

My jaw dropped. I pushed it shut with my fist. So Eve had slapped the stuffing out of Adam. That put a different spin on it. If a kiss equaled a base hit, then a slap was a strike.

I wanted to know more, like what happened after her slap, but there was no way to hear the rest of her story since the bell rang right then. The raucous roar of a class change drowned us out. I'd have to wait.

As usual, I ran into Adam in the dressing room. He seemed pleased with himself, but didn't he always?

"Why'd you leave the dance so early, Josh."

"I didn't feel well."

"Too bad. I had a cosmic time. I looked after Eve for you."

"I'm sure you did." I resisted the urge to give him a single-digit salute.

"Yeah. She's quite a girl. Just so you know, I got to first base with her."

"You did?"

"You weren't around, so I made my pitch."

"Did she play ball?" I wanted to hear Adam's version.

"A major leaguer. That girl's got a hot pair of lips."

He was trying to snow me, only I owned a snowplow. I could've said that Eve told me the rest of the story, but I didn't. I'd hold onto what I knew till the right moment. In the meantime, I'd give him something to think about.

Adam finished tying his shoes and got up to leave when I threw out an old gag of Abraham Lincoln's. "Hey," I said. "If you call a tail a leg, how many legs does a dog have?"

He hesitated, recognizing a trick question. I almost heard the whirring sound as his brain cells tried to compute the answer. He hesitated before offering the obvious answer, "Five?"

"Why, Adam, I'm surprised. I thought you were smarter than that."

"So, how many legs does this dumb dog of yours have?"

"Only four. Calling a tail a leg doesn't make it one." I looked him straight in the face and laughed.

"What was that all about?" He'd sensed some message in my joke but couldn't make it out.

"Think about it," I called over my shoulder as I jogged toward the gym.

Adam's not good with subtle stuff. Hints go over his head. Still, saying he'd gotten to first base with Eve didn't make it so. He could brag all he liked, but I knew Eve wasn't in love with him. But what were her feelings for me?

I wished for some sign she shared my feelings. Anything to show I wasn't standing alone in the cold. I remembered what Mom said about unrequited love. No wonder the Romans reserved a separate place down below where souls suffering from it could hang out together. Misery does love company.

I thought of Adam again, how confident he'd been about getting to first base. He didn't see it as a lie. Probably expected Eve to slap him. No doubt other girls had done the same. At first protested but then, finally, fell under his spell and into his arms. What for Eve meant rejection, only psyched him up for the next inning. Who was I to say he was wrong?

It worried me that he hadn't got her message, that he would continue his pursuit and, so long as he was putting the pressure on, it would distract her attention from me. I might not be as brave and bold as Adam, but I stuck to my guns when needed.

In some ways I was stronger than he was. I didn't change directions as often. When I charted a course, I stuck to it, whereas he was easily distracted. If a girl he'd never seen before showed up in school the next day and he liked her looks, he'd set his sights on this new target.

A comforting thought, but not one to count on. Wishing Lady Luck would look my way was like waiting to win the lottery. Could it happen? Sure, but the odds were unreal.

I needed a game plan. Putting my mind in motion, I entertained a number of notions, remembering that the simplest solution is often the best. It didn't take long to realize that the answer was right at hand.

Dad said girls liked boys who shared their feelings with them. So, if girls liked boys to be open, honest, and up front with them, then that's exactly what I'd be.

Wouldn't be easy. I understood that. I'd have to leave my

comfort zone, but discomfort was worth the effort if it worked.

I wouldn't be dishonest or anything like that. Adam could use the physical. I would use psychology.

In our upcoming study sessions Eve and I would be alone several afternoons a week. We'd be concentrating on class assignments, but there'd be breaks when we'd chat, joke, and share some scuttlebutt about school.

It'd be the perfect time to become better acquainted. I'd have the opportunity to open up a little, share my thoughts and feelings. If Eve liked what she heard, maybe she'd learn to like me, *really* like me, and we'd become a couple.

Was it realistic? I didn't know. But it seemed the only chance I had.

I beat Adam to the bus that afternoon and nestled beside Eve on a rear seat. "When do you want to start our study sessions?" I asked. I didn't let on I was pawing the ground like a stallion ready to race out of the starting gate.

"My mother always tells me there's no time like the present. Anything wrong with today?"

"I'll consult my calendar," I said, opening my notebook. "Only tea with the Queen of England at 4:00. But I can put her off."

"Good. That's settled. I'm in a panic over this English assignment. You're sure you can put me on the right path?"

"No problem. And this algebra that's sinking my grade point average, you'll bail me out?"

"Bailed out and under full sail. But I'll warn you, just because I understand it doesn't mean it'll be easy."

"I know. English, too. I may have made it sound too simple. I enjoy writing, but I also work at it."

"As long as you show me how to start, I'll put the time in."

"Same for me. Nothing's so hard that teamwork won't make easier."

"And it always helps to have a shoulder to cry on."

"I second that motion. Let me run home and write a note so my folks will know where I am. Then I'll come right over."

"Great. See you in a few minutes."

As I headed for home, Adam approached me. "Want to come over to my place and practice our catching?"

"Thanks, but I can't. Maybe another day. Something's come up."

I tried to sound mysterious, make him wonder what I was up to, but it failed. Adam's not the inquisitive type. He takes things at face value.

I considered telling him that Eve and I were study partners. See how he reacted. Then thought better of it. Eve could tell him if she wanted, but I doubted she did.

Knowing Adam, he'd probably invite himself to study with us. I'd lose my time alone with Eve, which was my hidden purpose. His presence would not only undermine that but also turn our meetings into nonstop foolishness. The longer he was in the dark, the better. Adam could learn about us later. Much later. Like after Eve had fallen in love with me.

I scribbled a brief note to Mom, telling her where I'd be. She got home around 5:00, but with Dad there was no telling. They liked to know where I'd be when I didn't have sports to occupy my afternoons. Now I had something more attractive to do.

I grabbed a bag of cookies from the pantry so I could suggest a break in our work. It's when we'd talk and get to know each other. To say I was excited about putting phase one of my plan into operation would be an understatement.

Eve must've seen me coming since she opened the door before I knocked. We spread our books and papers on the dining table, ready to work. I laid Scott on the sofa for his afternoon nap.

"Where do we start?" she asked.

"With you. Ladies always come first."

"A real gentleman."

"Thanks. My mom would be pleased to hear that."

I won't recount all I did to help Eve with her English paper, but basically it involved organization. She selected a topic that sounded interesting and then I went over things like research, note taking, outlining, rough drafts, and bibliographies. The actual writing would come later.

Eve's smile showed she felt better about the assignment and that meant I'd done a decent job. If she did the same for me, I might pass algebra after all. But, at that moment, we needed a break.

"I brought some chocolate cookies. What do you have to wash them down?"

"There are sodas in the fridge. Take your pick."

I selected a canned drink while she put some of the cookies on a plate, grabbed a couple of paper napkins, and put them on a table by the pool.

"The water looks inviting," I said.

"You can swim if you like."

"In what? I didn't bring a suit."

"That didn't seem to bother Adam the first time the three of us were here."

"Yeah? Well, Adam's got more nerve than me. He'd swim in nothing rather than go home in sopping wet clothes."

"I believe he would."

We were alone together and all we could talk about was Adam. I couldn't escape the guy, physically or mentally. He was like one of those bad dreams that keep coming back.

"Tell me if I'm being nosy, but why did you slap Adam at Friday night's dance?"

"To put him in his place."

"Why's that?"

"Because he doesn't own me. If I want a kiss, I'll ask for it."

"Then why did you go in there with him? You must've known what he was up to."

"I wasn't out of town when the brains were divided up."

"So?"

"I wanted to get it over with. I've had experience with guys like Adam. They think 'No' means 'Maybe' and 'Maybe' means 'Yes,' and they don't go away. I needed to send him a message, so I did."

"I'll say. Do you think he got it?"

"Partly. He's too high on himself to believe any girl could actually reject him."

"Then you think he'll try again?"

"You can bet on it."

I studied Eve's face. She was calm, convinced she could handle Adam. I liked that she knew her own mind, that she could take care of herself. She wasn't flighty, silly, or flirty but mature and adult.

It was then I saw what Adam said he'd seen in Eve when we first met her. He'd said she was the kinda girl who might let the right guy go all the way. I didn't believe him then, but I did now.

Not that she was wild or promiscuous. Simply, if she decided she wanted to do something, she would. She'd have thought it out. Every detail.

I asked myself, "Was that why I liked her?" I thought it was because she was curvy and cute, but now I saw much more. I liked her spirit and independence more than her looks. We were alike in some ways, or I liked to think so. I decided to learn all I could about Eve.

"What will you do when he does?" I asked. "Make another try, I mean."

"Keep letting him know I don't want any part of what he's got in mind."

"Adam's determined."

"He's met his match in me."

"I believe you. So why do you act like you like him?"

"It's no act. I do like him."

"You do?"

"Sure. Only not the way he wants. Adam's a great guy. He's

fun to be with. I want us to be friends, nothing more."

"You'll break his heart," I kidded, pretending to wipe a tear from my eye.

"He'll survive."

Eve was right. He'd survive. Adam would be shocked not to get to first base like he bragged, much less to home plate, but I had faith he'd find consolation in another girl's arms.

I felt better knowing how Eve felt about Adam. I could quit competing with him, relax, be myself. Not the old shy me, but a more confident and outgoing guy. One I was already learning to like.

I looked at my watch. Five o'clock. I scooped up my books in one arm and Scott in the other.

"We didn't get to your algebra problems, Josh. Let's start with them tomorrow."

"Okay, but be ready. You don't know how much I don't know."

"You can't be that bad."

"Wait and see."

I'd reached the sidewalk when I heard Eve call, "Josh."

"Yes?"

"Bring your bathing suit tomorrow. We'll go for a swim."

Chapter Ten

So I did. I brought the Speedo I wore when I swam, briefly, on a league team in seventh grade. I gave it up 'cause practice was a bore. Watching grass grow is more exciting and, with the super-chlorinated water in public pools, I smelled liked clothes washed in a gallon of bleach. After hours in the water I looked like a prune.

Swimming does develop strong chest and leg muscles, which is why I went out for the team in the first place. I envied swimmers' well-developed pecs that impress girls at the beach or under a tight tee shirt. What it took to get that lifeguard look wasn't worth it.

I toted my old team suit to Eve's for several reasons. One, it's light and fit in a jean pocket. Two, it dried fast. But if you want the real reason, it looked sexy.

Speedos fit snug and tight. There's not an overabundance of material 'cause in a race you don't want anything to slow you down.

I'd never worn the suit anywhere but swim practice 'cause it felt like strolling around in your underpants. My boxers cover more of me than the Speedo, but at an indoor pool with only guys it felt okay.

I suppose not wearing it in mixed company was another side to my shyness. I don't have anything to be ashamed of when it comes to how I'm built. When I compare myself to boys in the locker room, I stack up fine. Everyone wants to change something about their looks, like my wanting to have swimmers' pecs. I'll never be Mr. Universe, or want to, but my body's decent enough. It's feeling comfortable in my own skin that I need to work on.

Eve's pool seemed the best place to try out the new attitude I wanted to sell myself. I felt more relaxed around her than any girl I'd ever known. Even if nothing happened between us, I'd be ready for another girl in the future. This fear of letting myself go had to be ditched.

I won't say I whipped algebra but, with Eve's help, I put up a good fight. It was harder not concentrating on Eve than concentrating on the equations. I wished she'd lean over and kiss me again, but not on the cheek. I was afraid if I tried it I'd get slapped like Adam.

We did make progress, and I do mean we. Eve said after explaining the problems to me, they made more sense to her. Mom says you know you understand something when you can teach it to someone else.

Once I could explain to Eve exactly how to solve the assigned problems, she suggested we knock off for the day.

"Feel like a dip in the pool?"

"Sure, if you'll join me."

"Of course. You bring a suit?"

"Yep." I patted my pocket.

"You can change in the guest bath down the hall."

"Okay. I'll see you at the pool."

Men and women are alike in many ways and different in others, and one of the mysteries of life is why it takes females longer to dress or undress than it does males. Dad always complains when Mom's not on time to leave for a party. It's probably 'cause they care more about how they look than men do. Plus there's makeup and jewelry and dresses that zip up the back.

I pictured Eve getting undressed in her room, and that slowed me down a bit but, still, I was out of my clothes and into my swimsuit in under a minute. Before heading to the pool, I paused to check myself out in the mirror. My reflection gave me a jolt. I'd grown since swim team days, no longer the boy I'd been in seventh grade. There was more of me all around and no more of the Speedo. If it covered little of me then, it covered less now.

I tried stretching it, and that helped some, but there wasn't enough material to go around. I turned my back to the mirror, twisted my head to look, and saw my ass crack on display.

Damn! Decision time. Swim as I was or go home?

I decided to stay and swim. Tough it out. I'd take advantage of the time difference between men and women changing clothes to reach the pool before Eve. If I dived straight in, the water would conceal what my skimpy suit revealed.

I rushed down the hall and through the family room

without being seen and, clumsily, made more of a belly flop than a dive into the deep end. Thankfully Eve didn't witness my sorry performance.

I treaded water to warm up and did a few quick laps. You can't achieve real speed in a backyard pool 'cause it's not long enough, making you turn too often.

I stopped at the steps, stuck my head up, and saw Eve. I felt like Adam, and I don't mean my friend of that name, but the first man from the Garden of Eden. I understood how he felt seeing a woman for the first time. My Eve wasn't in a totally natural state, but her bikini-clad body left little to my imagination.

"Don't look at me like that," she said.

"Why not? You look great."

"Thanks, but I've not worn this suit before and I'm a bit embarrassed."

"You shouldn't be."

"Well, I am."

"You have nothing to be ashamed of."

"That has nothing to do with it. It's not how you look on the outside but how you feel on the inside."

My natural inclination said keep quiet, but I remembered what Dad said about girls liking guys who share their feelings.

"It's funny you should say that."

"Why?"

"I mean the coincidence of it. I feel the same way myself."

"About how you look?"

"Not *how* I look. More like how much *skin* my Speedo

shows. It's mucho smaller than the board shorts I usually wear swimming."

It wasn't fair to leave Eve standing before me while I concealed my body underwater. She smiled when I climbed out of the pool. "You're right. There's nothing baggy about that bathing suit."

I snapped the elastic against my skin. "Fits like a glove."

She looked at the team logo stitched on the side. "I didn't know you were on a swim team."

"In seventh grade. But not for long."

"Weren't you any good?"

"Average. I could've been better, but I hated its dullness. Baseball is way more exciting."

"What I like about swimming is the world's shut out when you're underwater. I feel so free. Nothing to think of but breathing and making the same strokes over and over."

"When did you buy the threads you're wearing?"

"As soon as we moved to Florida, so I'd fit into the tropical scene. It is called the Sunshine State."

"That's our motto."

"The one-piece suits my swim team wore were ugly. I wanted something sexier."

"You succeeded."

"You don't think it exposes too much?"

"Not for me."

She laughed. "It's okay here, but I'd feel uncomfortable around strangers."

"Same here. I'm trying to get over my shyness."

Eve laughed again. "You? Shy? Can't be wearing that. Besides, boys don't have to hide as much as girls."

"Maybe not, but we still worry about how we look."

"Really?"

"Really."

"I thought it was only girls."

"Step in the boy's bathroom and watch us jostle for mirror space."

"I'll take your word for it."

"Maybe guys don't use makeup and stuff, but we still want to look good to girls."

Eve remained silent for a minute, thinking, then asked, "Do boys think about girls as much as girls think about boys?"

"I dunno. How often do girls think about boys?"

"Maybe a hundred times a day."

"We've got you beat. Girls are all we think about."

"Even asleep?"

I blushed, remembering my wet dream. "Let's not go there. It can get embarrassing."

"I think I know what you mean."

"You do?"

"The girl's coach covered boy's bodies last week when we were separated for sex education."

"That's not fair."

"Why not. Didn't your coach talk about what happens to girls each month?"

"Well, yeah."

"Shouldn't we both know how the opposite sex operates?"

"Of course, only I've never talked about sex with a girl."

"Most of us are shy about it. We should be more open and honest with the opposite sex."

"Yeah, you're right." I considered what she said and got an idea. "Hey, Eve, why don't we share what's talked about in our separate sex-ed sessions. You tell me what's on girls' minds and I'll fill you in on the boys."

"Deal."

"Then we'll add sex to our English and algebra agenda."

Eve flashed a big smile. "Okay, but only talk. No experiments."

I blushed again, wishing for the thousandth time I could control it.

Seeing my embarrassment, Eve said, "Let's cool off. This talk's getting kinda hot."

KERSPLOOSH! I did a cannonball into the pool, spraying water all over her. As I came up for air she jumped in and we had a full-scale water battle. Laughing and gasping for breath, we collapsed on the steps. I liked being with her and it seemed she enjoyed being with me.

As we sat there, side by side, I thought of it as my first date. I'd been to dances and parties, but I'd never been on a "date" date. Not where I'd asked a girl to go out with me, only the two of us, having fun being together.

Eve threw me a towel. After drying off, I wrapped it around my waist.

"Still feeling exposed in your Speedo?"

"Yeah, a little. And you?"

"Better. I'm glad it's you here and not Adam."

"Why's that?"

"It's the way he looks at me. Makes me feel undressed even when I'm fully covered. What would he do if he saw me like this?"

"I see what you mean."

"Thanks. You're a gentleman, Josh."

I wasn't sure I wanted to be a gentleman. I'd rather be more like Adam. I wanted to take her in my arms and kiss her like he'd have done. Hold her tightly and feel her lips on mine. There was more I wanted to do, but Eve was right. I couldn't help being a gentleman.

After I dressed I got my books and woke Scott from his nap. Eve came out in a robe. I wondered if she was naked under it. Her damp hair was brushed straight back, giving her a fashion-model look. I'd never seen a girl so gorgeous, and there I was, alone with her.

"Earth to Josh. Do you read me? Come in please."

"Sorry. What?"

"A penny for your thoughts."

"A penny wouldn't buy much."

"You looked miles away."

"I was thinking," I said, but I didn't say what.

"Can I ask something personal?"

"Okay." Here was a chance to overcome my shyness.

"If your swimsuit made you feel embarrassed, why did you wear it?"

"It's easy to carry." I pulled it out of my pocket. "And it

dries fast."

"No other reason?"

"Maybe one more."

"And that is?"

"You want me to admit it?"

"Come clean."

"All right. I wanted you to notice me."

"When haven't I noticed you?"

"I'm not talking about normal noticing."

"What kind then?"

"You know."

"Tell me."

"You want a full confession?"

"The whole truth and nothing but."

"I wanted to look sexy. Satisfied?"

"Yes."

"I could ask you the same question."

"And you'd get the same answer."

"Great minds think alike, huh?"

"I don't know about the 'great' part, but teenager's minds tend to think alike."

"How do you think we scored in the looking sexy contest?"

"An A+."

"I agree."

Eve's face was stern. "Listen carefully, Josh. I have something important to say before you go."

"Okay." I was half afraid to hear what was coming next.

"You've got great buns." Eve laughed and her face lit up

with a brilliant smile.

She took me totally by surprise, like the Indians took General Custer. Funny thing was, I didn't blush this time.

"Thanks. I could return the compliment."

"What's stopping you?"

I felt my shyness slip away as I took a deep breath and looked straight into her eyes. "Eve, you've got great buns."

Chapter Eleven

I wore a mile-wide grin all the way home, pleased with myself in more ways than one. I'd overcome some of my shyness, thanks to Eve. She made me feel relaxed and comfortable when I was with her, and I found it easier to talk honestly about things that embarrassed me before. Last and least, I actually understood the "X's" and "Y's" of an algebra assignment. Life was good.

I'd traveled a long way from my old self. I felt new and improved. No going back. The more I opened up, the easier it got. And the easier it got, the more ready I became to open up some more. And I owed it all to one lovely lady.

She might not love me as I loved her, but I could wait. We belonged together. No mistake. It'd all work out in time. A surge of that self-confidence Adam's famous for flowed through me. For a minute I feared I'd explode.

I knew Eve liked me. But she liked Adam, too. She'd said as much. I was quieter, easier going than him. Not that he wasn't a gentleman. He was a good guy. But he was putting pressure on Eve and couldn't see she didn't like it.

He'd never run into a girl that independent. I tried to think of a single girl in school who wouldn't have welcomed a little pressure from Adam. And there Eve was, giving him thumbs down, but he was too high on himself to see it.

I did some thinking as I walked home. Where it came from I couldn't say but, somewhere inside me, I had the feeling Eve was hiding something. A little voice I'd never heard before whispered in my ear, "There's more here, Josh, than meets the eye."

Eve had two guys wild about her. I wanted her to cut Adam and choose me. He wanted the opposite. Yet she acted like we were nothing but friends without serious feelings for her.

It didn't make much sense, but that's how I felt. I'd lost my senses over Eve. My brain ran on empty while my hormones had a full tank of the high-octane stuff.

On the bus the next morning Adam monopolized Eve, but I wasn't worried. I had her every afternoon all to myself alone, and he didn't have a clue. Would I clue him in? No way.

Since I'd see Eve at lunch, I left her with Adam and went straight to the media center to work on an English assignment before the first bell. I'd barely opened my notebook when Amy Lynne ambushed me. From the shock of seeing her, I swallowed my gum. The media center wasn't her usual hangout, and I don't think she'd recognize a book if it bit her.

Amy Lynne preferred roaming the mall in her free hours, while at school she squandered her time wandering the halls with the chatterbox chicks. So I was super surprised when she spoke to me.

"Hey, Josh, got a sec?"

"Yeah. What's up?"

"You're Adam's best friend."

"I don't know about best, but we're friends."

"And you hang out with the new girl, Eve?"

I nodded, wondering if she'd ever get to the point, if she had one.

"So, like, you know, does she like Adam?"

"The three of us are friends, if that's what you mean." But I knew she meant much more than that. Still, I enjoyed stringing her along.

"You know what I mean."

"You mean does she LIKE him?"

"Yeah. Are they going steady?"

"Not that I know."

"You're sure?"

"Sure I'm sure. You think they'd slip that past me?"

She considered it, cocked her head to one side, thought a moment, and finally said, "I just wanted to make sure. You are being straight with me, Josh? You wouldn't lie?"

"Cross my heart."

"Thanks." The muscles of her face relaxed as she gave a small sigh of relief.

In my super shy days I would've left it at that. But now I stuck my neck out. "Amy Lynne," I called out as she walked away. "Who told you Adam was going steady with Eve?"

"Friends."

"Real friends wouldn't shovel you a load of manure

like that."

"Guess not."

"They say where they got it from?"

"I dunno. It's all over school. Think they made it up?"

"Wouldn't surprise me. Some kids are good at making up stories."

"You're right about that."

She'd probably done the same. I felt like saying, "It takes one to know one," instead I said, "Trust me. It's not true."

"It still hurts."

I saw a pained look on her face and started to feel sorry for her. "You really care about Adam, don't you?"

"More than any boy I've ever known. I'd do anything to get him to like me." Amy Lynne stared at me a second, probably wondering if she should trust me. "Hey, Josh. Adam listens to you. Tell him how I feel. Okay?"

"Why don't you?"

"I tried."

"And?"

"That's when he kissed me in front of all the kids in our lunch period. Didn't you hear about it?"

"Yeah, Adam told me. So what happened after that?"

"Eve happened."

"Oh."

"So, will you? Tell him I mean. About how I feel."

"I'll think about it."

The first bell cut our conversation short. If she said anything after that, I missed it. But I kept my promise. I thought about if or how I'd give Adam her love message. She'd fallen hard while he only had eyes for Eve.

I didn't tell Amy Lynne I knew how she felt. Probably wouldn't believe me. But it was true. We were both in a boat called "Unrequited Love."

Should I start a club? Gather together all those lovers whose love was unreturned. I pictured our meetings. Everyone crying on each other's shoulders. Not a cheery thought.

My thoughts about Amy Lynne's request seesawed. She'd already told Adam her feelings for him. What good could I do? He'd think I was trying to get him off Eve's scent.

Adam might be a joker, but he was no dummy. I'd need a swifter move than that to turn his attention from Eve. Problem was, I didn't have a swift move at hand.

My brain cells scanned the empty shelves. Then, Bingo! I remembered what Amy Lynne said. What were her exact words? "Let him know how I feel." What else? Oh, yes, she liked him "more than any boy I've ever known." More important, "I'd do anything to get him to like me." *Anything*? Was that the message she wanted delivered?

If it was, did she mean it? Was she willing to put out to get him? Only Amy Lynne could answer that question.

I saw the advantage to me. I could quit competing with Adam, relax around Eve, and let things move at their own sweet speed.

Eve had already heard the rumor about Adam and her going steady. She'd told me it wasn't true. Would she care what Amy Lynne said or did? Probably not. Still, it couldn't hurt to bring her up to speed. Or could it?

At lunch my mind got diverted from Adam and Amy Lynne to how Eve looked in that bikini, especially when wet, and the sexy little mole on her right shoulder. I remembered every inch of her. Then she broke into my daydream.

"What's on your mind, Josh? You look like you're miles away."

"What? Oh, nothing important. But I could use your advice."

"Okay."

"Amy Lynne wants me to give Adam a message, and I don't know if I should."

"What is it?"

"That she likes him more than any other boy."

"He's probably figured that out already."

"That's not all."

"What else?"

"That she'd do anything to get him to like her."

"Interesting."

"Think she means it?"

"Dunno. What do you think?"

"I think she does. She sounded desperate."

"Is that anything new? Haven't they been a couple before?"

"Off and on. But now she's worried about you."

"Me?"

"Yes, you."

"She's crazy."

"Maybe, but she says the scuttlebutt still has you and Adam

going steady."

I squirmed like there were ants in my pants when I said it. How would Eve react? Not well, I figured. Like putting a match to a cherry bomb, and Eve's fuse was short. Her explosion reached me before I could cover my ears. I won't repeat her exact words.

"Don't get excited."

"Is that crap still making the rounds? If I get my hands on whoever's spreading that story, they're gonna be a few more notches down the food chain."

"Don't get bent out of shape," I said, taking one of her hands in mine.

"Easy for you to say. Your reputation's not at stake."

"No. But the bigger deal you make of it, the more kids will think it's true."

"I suppose. Still . . ." Her facial muscles began to relax as she calmed down.

"I know. A bummer. My advice is, ignore it."

"I will, right after Mr. Adam and I have a face-to-face."

I tried to cheer her up with some of my father's light bulb jokes. It didn't work, but Eve must've appreciated my attempt 'cause, as we were leaving, she laid a hand on my shoulder and said, "You're sweet, Josh."

Why couldn't Adam move to Timbuktu? Why did he have to come between me and the only girl I really cared for? We were meant for each other. If only the world would get out of our way so she could discover the deep love I had for her.

When I saw Adam in science lab, I gave him fair warning.

"Eve's gunning for you."

"She's already shot me down."

"What do you mean."

"She caught up with me between classes."

"And?"

"My plane went down in flames. But I parachuted to safety."

"Don't be so cryptic."

The teacher shot us a can-the-chitchat-and-get-to-work look.

"Later," he whispered. "On the bus. I'll tell you then."

Chapter Twelve

My attention wasn't on science that day. I tried mental telepathy to make the classroom clock run faster. Einstein might've managed it, but not an eighth grader. Suddenly, our teacher's surprise proclamation snapped me out of my daydream.

"I've decided to call a halt to our parenting experiment," she said.

Before the last word escaped her mouth, the class cheered. We were so loud the teacher next door stuck his head in our room.

"I take it you're not disappointed?"

A chorus of "No's" echoed off the walls.

"So, how did it feel to be a parent?"

One boy said, "Like being in jail."

"You found it confining?"

"Yeah," a girl said. "I couldn't do some fun things I like."

"Baby sitting's a drag, huh?"

"I'll say," another girl said. "It's a twenty-four-seven. Never ending."

"Too much responsibility," a boy added. "It was neat at first, but then I got sick of it."

"Did it make you appreciate your parents more?"

The whole class laughed when Adam said, "I don't know how they put up with me. Parenting's a pooper."

"Any other ideas?"

A quiet girl raised her hand. "We only experienced the part that's hard work. A real baby's different."

"How is it different, Cassandra?"

"Well, a real baby is yours. It's someone who can't live without your care and love. And it loves you back."

"You're saying it's difficult to have feelings for a sack of flour?"

"Yeah. If you love a baby, then you take care of it. You don't mind the hard work."

The teacher nodded her head. "That's very true."

Another girl said, "I wouldn't mind caring for someone's baby, but I know I'm not ready to have one of my own yet."

"Anyone have another thought to add?"

"I want to get my career started first," someone else added. "I learned you shouldn't have a baby until you're able to support one."

A boy waved his hand. "Why are you ending the experiment early?"

"Because you've learned in a small way what a big job it is caring for a baby. Look around if you want another reason. Most of your babies can't take much more of your attention."

Scott had held up pretty well. I'd kept him wrapped in a soft, blue blanket, but many babies were in sad shape.

One flour sack was covered in Band-Aids, another was held together with duct tape. One boy caught in a thunderstorm had a gooey mess wrapped in plastic. Adam had lost track of Rose somewhere in the mall. If these were real babies I'd have dialed 911.

We'd learned that babies are a serious business. It requires maturity and responsibility to raise them properly. I'd also learned I was a long way from ready to be a father.

At the end of class I deposited my sack on the counter with a mixture of sadness and relief. "Bye, Scott," I whispered. "I'll miss you."

"That was a weird teaching trick," Adam said as we walked to the bus.

"Then I wish more teachers were weird. I learned a lot more carting Scott around than I'd get from a film, lecture, or book."

"Maybe, but it was still kinda hokey."

"If you'd spent a little more time and attention on Rose, you might've learned more."

"I'm a busy man. I have my career to think of."

"The only career you have is girls."

"Can you think of a better one?"

Considering that we were both eighth-grade boys, he had a point. Instead of agreeing with him, I said, "You promised to tell all about your run-in with Eve."

"Crash is the word for it."

"Why was she upset?"

"Some crazy rumor that we're going steady."

"Again! Did you start this one, too?"

"I was only trying to make Amy Lynne jealous."

"You hit the jackpot."

He stopped suddenly, giving me his full attention. "How so?"

I debated with myself. An angel whispered advice in one ear and a devil in the other. After a brief struggle, the devil won.

"She told me."

"No kidding?"

"She's crazy about you."

"Isn't everyone?"

"Adam, please, have a *little* modesty."

"What did she say?"

"That she'd do anything to get you."

"*Anything*?"

"Straight from the horse's mouth."

"My plan worked."

"What plan?"

"A little double play I plotted. One where I'll score with Eve and Amy Lynne at the same time."

"Please explain, honored master," I said, bowing from the waist. "Your humble student awaits instruction in your mysterious powers over women."

"It's called playing hard to get. I don't have the right number for Eve. All I get is a dial tone. So I'll ignore her for a while. When she sees I've gone back to Amy Lynne, she'll wish she hadn't brushed me off."

"And rush into your open arms?"

"Something like that. Meanwhile, Amy Lynne's so jealous of Eve she's ready to go the distance to get me back."

"All the way, you mean?"

"We'll see. How serious did she sound?"

"Serious squared."

Adam grinned. "If I play my cards right, I'll get an 'A+' on my sex education homework."

"You've never done a night's homework in your life."

"I never had this kind before."

"But they don't want us to actually practice what they're teaching about sex. Not yet anyway."

"Why bother learning something if you don't put it to good use?"

"Your point being?"

"I don't plan to wait so long that I forget what they've taught us."

"Strike while the iron is hot, huh?"

"Exactly. Except I hope it's Amy Lynne who's hot."

"And you think Eve will react the same way?"

"I plan to find out. Girls can't stand to be ignored."

The same was true for boys, or at least it was for me. If you like someone, any attention feels fine. The worst is when a girl acts like you don't even exist.

Adam was faking about his great plan. I knew him too well. Seen him act like he'd won when he'd actually lost. Since Eve brushed him off, he was going back to the first girl who put out the welcome mat.

Amy Lynne was pissed off about being ignored, too, so they

were gonna get it together again, out of frustration more than anything else. I only hoped they wouldn't do something stupid they'd regret later.

"Listen, Adam. Sex is a powerful force. Don't do anything crazy you'll pay for the rest of your life."

"Listen yourself. This is a subject I know something about. I haven't given my attention to math, English, or history but, once the sex-ed lessons started, I never missed a word. I'm a walking encyclopedia when it comes to the do's and don'ts and how's and why's."

"I believe you. It's just that things can get out of control pretty fast. Think about it."

"I will."

"Promise?"

He raised his right hand as if taking an oath. "I swear to take every precaution." Then he patted his jeans pocket where he probably kept a condom.

"Later, Josh. I'm gonna see if I can sneak a ride on Amy Lynne's bus."

"How will you get home? Doesn't she live on the other side of the interstate?"

"Love will find a way," he called over his shoulder as he raced off.

When I joined Eve on the bus, she asked, "Where's Adam off to so fast? He'll miss his ride."

"In search of Amy Lynne. Whatever you told him today must've made its way through his thick skull. He's decided to play hard to get."

"With me?"

"Yep. He thinks you'll get jealous when you see him with another girl."

"And beg him to come back?"

"You got it."

"You have to admire the guy. He's an ocean of optimism."

"What did you tell him? Today, I mean. He said he ran into you in the hall."

"What didn't I tell him? I laid my message on him clear and loud."

"Which was?"

"You want the long or the short version?"

"The short."

"That he had a snow cone's chance on a summer's day."

"Hard to mistake that."

"I hope so, for my sake."

I considered her last comment. There was more to Eve's rejection of Adam than I could see. It was the way she said, "for my sake," that made me wonder. My shyness didn't want to ask a personal question, but I overcame it.

"Eve, tell me it's none of my business, but I have to ask you something."

"You can ask, but I won't promise to answer."

"Fair enough. I've just got to figure out how to say it."

"Spit it out. Whatever it is you're thinking."

"Okay. I feel like I'm missing something. Aren't you coming down on Adam pretty hard?"

"You mean overreacting?"

"Yeah, like overkill."

Eve looked thoughtful, serious. She didn't seem upset. More nervous than anything. She'd agreed to my asking but didn't promise an answer. I watched her chew on a fingernail.

"I'll tell you about it, Josh, but not here. Wait till we're home. My place, I mean."

We never got around to studying that afternoon. We talked—openly, honestly, sharing thoughts and feelings.

As soon as we were settled, Eve began. "I don't know where you got the idea there was something behind me being so hard on Adam. More than just not wanting to go with him. Acting upset and all."

"I don't know myself. Somehow it didn't seem like you."

"Well, there's a reason. A good one."

Eve paused. I waited.

"There was a boy in Atlanta I really liked. He was fun loving like Adam. They're a lot alike."

She stopped. I felt a stab of jealousy over a guy I'd never seen.

"So, Adam reminds you of an old boyfriend? Is that why you don't want to get close to him?"

"Partly."

The way Eve said that one little word meant much more was left unsaid.

"You miss that boy, right?"

"Wrong."

"Wrong?"

"About like I'd miss getting a tooth pulled."

"Didn't the guy like you?" I wondered if this was another case of unrequited love.

"Oh, he *liked* me all right."

I didn't like the way she said, "*liked*."

"He liked you. You liked him. What more could you want?"

"A lot."

"For instance?"

"Like respect."

"Respect?"

"Is that too much to expect?"

"No."

If we were getting anywhere, we were moving in slow motion. "Eve, if you're uncomfortable talking about this, don't say anything more."

"I'm sorry. It's still painful. But there's no reason you shouldn't know. That boy was a capital J, capital E, capital R, capital K."

"He was if he didn't respect you."

"Thanks. To make a short story shorter, we went together for a few months. Everything was fine, at first. Then he started pressuring me."

She paused for a moment. I nodded, letting her know I understood.

"I could see he didn't really like me for me. He only wanted to do *it* and figured I liked him enough to give in."

"What happened?"

"I asked what part of 'NO' he didn't understand. He got nasty and rough, then called me a few words I won't repeat."

"He didn't hit you, did he?"

"No, but I thought he might. He was high. I only knew I had to get out of there fast."

"What'd you do?"

"Called my dad to pick me up. We were at a party. A high school guy's house."

"Chaperones?"

"None."

"Beer?"

"Gallons, and other stuff. I should never have gone, but I felt honored to be invited. It seemed so sophisticated."

"I hope you didn't see him again."

"Of course not. I'm not stupid."

"Listen, Eve. I know Adam pretty well. He'd never act like that."

"I'm not through."

"There's more?"

"Lots."

"But you broke up with him."

"Yeah, I did. I thought that was the end of it, but the next day the stories started."

"Stories? What kinda stories?"

"Use your imagination, Josh."

"Oh! I see where this is going."

"I went into one of the bedrooms with him. Some girl opened the door and saw us kissing. When my date spread the word we'd done a lot more, everyone believed him."

She was close to tears but got control of herself. I waited

before going on.

"What did you do about it?"

"What could I do?"

"Tell the truth."

"I tried, but you know how kids are. They love to believe the worst."

I nodded in agreement. "I know."

"That slime spread all over school. Even some of my good friends bought the story. It was awful."

"I can imagine."

"The worst part was, boys came after me 'cause they thought I was 'easy.'"

Hearing the anger in Eve's voice made me mad. I wanted to hold, comfort, and protect her.

Eve turned and faced me. "Did I say that was the worst? Well, it wasn't. One of my teachers heard the gossip and called my mother. Told her she ought to keep a better eye on me."

"Jeez!"

"At least Mom believed me. We've always been open and honest with each other. Still, I knew that teacher would tell others. It made me sick to sit in class wondering what they were thinking." She stood up and began wandering slowly around the room.

"It must've been pure hell."

"It was. I was happy when Mom said we were moving here. I could leave all that garbage behind."

"I understand."

"Now can you see why the going-steady story that Adam

spread spooked me?"

"I can."

"I was afraid of going through the same thing again."

"That's natural." I felt we needed to return to where we were before, back to happier times. Then the first joke I'd ever made up myself came to me out of nowhere.

"Hey, Eve. How many light bulbs does take to change a flat tire?"

She gave me a Mr. Spock's one-eyebrow-raised, quizzical look.

"Give up?"

"I can't even guess."

"Only one. As long as it's not too dark."

For the first time that afternoon Eve smiled. A smile of relief to get it all out, to share her pain with a friend.

"Thanks for the joke, Josh. And for listening, too. You're the only one I would tell that to."

"You know I'm always here for you, Eve."

"Thanks, Josh. That means a lot."

"No more serious stuff. Let's have our swim."

Chapter Thirteen

I woke the next morning with Adam and Amy Lynne on my mind. Did he catch up with her? Did he manage to sneak past her bus driver and hitch a ride to her house? If he did, I knew she'd let him in.

Amy Lynne was wise in the ways of boys. She might not know the story of the Trojan horse, but she'd know what Adam had in mind and what might happen if she opened the door to him. Was love or lust or both breathing so loudly she failed to see the warning signs? I've heard love is blind, but sometimes it's 'cause we shut our eyes.

Answers wouldn't come till science lab. If Adam was willing to tell all and, if so, would it all be true? By lunch I had some clues.

Rumors circulated in homeroom that Adam and Amy Lynne were an item again. Second period had them engaged and, by third, they'd set the date and booked a wedding chapel in Vegas.

It was a real-life game of Gossip where a simple story gets passed along and facts get mixed up 'cause people don't always listen well, or only hear what they want to hear, or even spice the story up to make it more interesting. The truth is never so interesting it can't be jazzed up.

In third grade our teacher told a kid she'd locked her keys in the car when it was really cold and, by the time help came, her teeth were chattering so much she couldn't talk clearly. That afternoon another kid told her he was sorry she'd caught a cold after locking her false teeth in her car.

If a story can get that mixed up by accident, imagine what happens to a juicy piece of scandal. As Eve said, kids like to believe the worst. I'd say adults do, too. They also enjoy passing it on after adding something extra.

If the stories kept multiplying, by last period I'd hear that Amy Lynne gave birth to twins, divorced Adam, and eloped with Elvis after meeting him in a Krispy Kreme. The wilder and weirder a rumor gets, the easier it seems to believe. I could sell a story about little green men landing their spaceship on the school roof to collect samples of cafeteria food for analysis before I'd get a single student to believe that lunchroom hamburgers don't contain a trace of real beef.

When I connected with Eve at lunch, a mob had gathered around Amy Lynne's usual table. I couldn't see her through the curious crowd that reminded me of vultures, picking every scrap of flesh from the bones of the story.

Knowing Amy Lynne, she loved the attention. Eve had been upset by such verbal diarrhea, but I knew Amy Lynne wasn't. She liked to be talked about, good or bad.

"Are you up-to-the-minute on the unfolding soap opera?"

I asked Eve.

"I'm not sure. Changes by the minute. Are they living together or still only going steady?"

I looked at my watch. "They may've vowed till death do us part by now. It's been thirty minutes since I heard the latest."

"We could join them," Eve said, pointing to Amy Lynne's table. "They're sure to be getting the latest straight from the horse's mouth."

"Doesn't mean you can trust it."

"True. But why would she want the school to think she and Adam hooked up?"

"She doesn't think like us. Amy Lynne wants kids to believe she jumped in the sack with Adam."

"Why?"

"The same reason kids try drinking or smoking. They think it makes them look grown up. How did you say going to that party with all the beer and stuff made you feel?"

"Sophisticated."

"There you are. When you try to impress other kids, it's easy to get in over your head."

"Josh, do you believe there's anything to all this talk?"

"Half hot air, I'd wager. I'll see Adam in science this afternoon. See what he says."

"Think he'll tell? The truth, I mean."

"Probably. We're pals. And Adam's not one to hide his light under a basket."

"But he's not above bragging how bright his light is either."

"True. I'll try to sort it all out and let you know."

Eve's eyes had a far-away, thinking-deep-thoughts look. I didn't like to pry, but I had to ask, "Are you okay?"

"What? Sorry. Yeah, I'm okay. I might even say happy."

"About what?"

"Can't you read my mind?"

"No, but I might come close if I guessed."

"Try."

"Here goes. You're glad the gossip isn't about you. Am I in the ballpark?"

"Yep, a clean hit."

"It may be an old-fashioned idea, but a gentleman doesn't kiss and tell."

"Nor does a lady."

"Are we the only ones who believe that?

"Probably."

"Nothing's sacred anymore."

"Certainly not sex."

I considered Eve's comment. We're swamped with the three-letter "S" word. It's everywhere—advertising, sitcoms, rock videos, films. Newspapers report rapes, molestation, and worse every morning. Stuff my dad says were never discussed when he was growing up are now tossed in front of six-year-olds.

Eve broke into my thoughts. "Looks like I'm not the only one who's serious."

"It's catching."

"Forgive me. I didn't mean to infect you."

"No problem. I'll get over it."

"Would a light bulb joke help? I just remembered one. Maybe your dad doesn't know it."

"It can't be worse than his. So, how many, fill in the blank, does it take to change a light bulb?"

"Ski instructors."

"Put me out of my misery."

"Four."

"Why four?"

"One to screw in the bulb and three to criticize the turns."

"YEEUCK!"

"C'mon, it's not that bad."

I stuck my finger down my throat, pretending to throw up.

"That's the last time I tell you a joke with a light bulb in it."

"Swear. Then sign in blood."

"Really, Josh. It wasn't *that* bad."

"I'm teasing. Actually, it's the first light bulb joke I've heard that's close to being funny."

"Thanks. If it didn't make you laugh, at least you don't look half so serious anymore."

"Your face has taken on a lighter look, too."

"Then it did us both good."

"Nothing wrong with that. See you on the bus."

"Later."

I missed Adam in the locker room but in science I punched him in the arm and said, "You old son-of-a-gun. Some wild stories about you are making the rounds."

He gave me a wink. "What can I say? People will talk."

"Not without a reason."

"Since when do they need a reason?"

"Okay, so they don't always need one. Do they have one this time?"

"You mean about me and you know who?"

"Who else? Fess up, Adam. This is your teammate talking. You must've told half the school by now."

"I've been as silent as study hall. Can I help it if I was seen going home with a certain young lady?"

"It's what happened *in* her home."

"Nosy, aren't we?"

"Don't keep me in suspense. Tell all."

"My lips are zipped."

"Since when? Nothing to talk about, huh? Just as I suspected."

"Oh, there's plenty to talk about. It's just that some things are better *not* talked about."

"I can't believe I'm hearing that from you."

"I'm not always a blabbermouth, you know."

"No, I didn't know."

"I may have run my mouth about stuff I wanted to do, but I'm not gonna write a column in the school paper about anything more."

"Then you're a true gentleman, Adam."

"Of sorts."

"Then where are the stories coming from?"

"The lady, I presume."

"It doesn't bother you?"

"It's a free country. She can say what she likes."

"We'd better get to work, or the teacher will say what she likes."

We did an admirable dissection job on an earthworm and, washing up, I finally raised the question I'd wanted to ask. It took all the courage I had.

"Adam?"

"Yeah?"

"About you and Eve?"

"What about us?"

"Are you still after her? You know, since whatever's going on between you and Amy Lynne."

"Josh, old boy, I struck out with Eve. The field's open for you."

"For me!"

"Don't sound so shocked. I know you're hot for her."

"I haven't said anything."

"You don't have to. It's written in ink on your face."

"That obvious?"

"I know the look of love when I see it. You've got it bad, haven't you?"

"About as bad as it gets."

"You want some advice?"

"Sure."

"Go for it."

"*It*?"

"A homerun."

"I don't know, Adam. Eve isn't Amy Lynne."

"Listen. I've seen how Eve looks at you. You're halfway to

home plate already."

"You think so?"

"Trust me."

"I don't know. I'd settle for going steady."

"That's so minor league. Try out for the majors."

"I'll think about it."

"Do that." He looked me straight in the eye. "I'll level with you on one thing, amigo."

"I'm listening."

"The difference between the majors and minors, it's the difference between day and night, between becoming a man and remaining a boy."

"Thanks for the tip."

"You're welcome. I'd like my friend to grow up with me."

"My body's ready, if my mind will buy it."

"Did you see that old Robin Williams movie on cable last weekend?"

"The one in the boarding school for boys?"

"Yep. Remember what he told them? That Latin thing."

"Carpe diem?"

"That's it. 'Seize the day.' Make the most of what you've got while you've got it. That's my new motto."

"I can buy that."

"Great. Give it a try. Live a little."

"I'll try, but isn't there something about curiosity killing the cat?"

"Yeah, and there's also something about satisfaction bringing it back."

As the class cleaned up from the lab, Adam disappeared. Plain vanished. Since no one seemed to notice, I kept my mouth shut.

As sure as one and one make two, I knew Adam had headed for Amy Lynne's room. He'd want to walk her to the bus and give her a goodbye kiss. He might even sneak another ride to her house. But that was his business. I had enough of my own.

First, the thing Adam said about Eve. How she looked at me. Did he imagine it? If she felt as I did, I'd do back flips down the hall.

On the bus Eve asked, "What'd you find out?"

I blinked. "About what?"

"Adam and Amy Lynne."

"Oh, them. Nothing. And everything."

"That's a big help."

"Sorry. I've been in a parallel universe."

"You do look spaced out. Want to talk about it."

"Later. Let me field your question first."

"Okay. How can you learn nothing and everything?"

"Adam isn't talking. That says a lot. I've never seen him clam up before."

"How can not talking say a lot?"

"'Cause he always exaggerates. He can't do that if he's quiet. I believe something significant happened between the two of them yesterday, that all the talk is on target. His silence says everything."

"You're not making sense, yet I think I understand."

"Are we crazy, or what?"

“Not crazy. Just on the same wave length.”

“I’ll settle for that. Hey, I’ve got an idea.”

“What?”

“Let’s not even pretend to do schoolwork this afternoon. We deserve a break. It’s good to goof off every now and then.”

“When did you become so smart?”

“Always have been. Just try to hide it. And don’t say I hide it well.”

“I don’t have to. You said it yourself.”

“Ouch!”

“Only joking. Come on over when you’re ready.”

“See you in a few minutes,” I said, not realizing how true those words would prove to be.

Chapter Fourteen

I batted around what Adam said in science lab. The part about me being halfway to home plate with Eve sounded good, if true. He couldn't know for sure. But I figured he did know about the difference between the major and minor leagues and going for a homerun.

He'd taken the long way round, not using the straight talk I always got from Adam. But I got his message. He'd gone from boy to man in one afternoon and thought I had an equal chance as well. The question was, how to get started?

As I walked up to Eve's front door, a line from an old Jimmy Buffet song came to mind. "I'll jump-start you if you will kick-start me." That'd help. To have Eve meet me part way.

To be real, failure frightened me. What wouldn't I give for some of Adam's self-confidence? I'd have to make it up as I went along.

We changed into our skimpy swimsuits and met at the pool where we sat side-by-side, legs dangling in the warm water, cold drinks in hand, making small talk. It was Eve who switched to the serious side.

"Didn't we say we'd share stuff from our sex education groups? You still want to?"

"I guess so, if it's not too personal. You wouldn't believe some of the crazy questions that guys ask."

"I might. Try me."

I felt my face turn red. "Why don't you start?"

"What do you want to know?"

"How about what worries girls most."

"Measurements. Mostly the chest." She cupped her hands in a suggestive way. "Girls who don't have much up front are afraid boys won't notice them."

"That's not entirely true."

"Gimme a break, Josh. You know that's the first place boys look."

"Okay, so we do. Maybe too much. But what does that have to do with your class?"

"You mentioned crazy questions. Well, one girl ordered some contraption to make her breasts bigger. Saw an ad in a magazine. She wanted to know how much longer she needed to use it before it worked."

"She really believed it?"

"Yeah. The coach explained these things are a rip-off, but I'm not sure the girl bought it."

"I've never seen one advertised."

"You don't read some women's magazines."

"No, not lately."

"It shows what girls will do to attract a boy."

"Wow!"

"That's my inside story. What's yours?"

"Boys have measurement worries, too."

"Not like ours."

"Why do you think I went in for swimming? I wanted a powerful chest. Boys lift weights for the same reason. Girls go for muscle men. I've seen you all ogle them and call them 'hunks.'"

"I don't care for too much muscle. I prefer a well-proportioned male body. Like yours."

"Mine?"

"You're put together pretty well."

I returned the compliment. "So are you."

"Thanks. Tell me a wild question from your class."

"I'm still thinking."

"You're stalling."

"Am not." But I was. How had a shy kid like me got in such an embarrassing spot? Then I imagined Adam whispering in my ear, "Go for it."

"It's close to the story you told."

"You mean like the thing that girl bought?"

"Yep, but for a different body part. One girls don't have."

"Uh oh. I'm seeing the picture."

"Boys worry about size, too. Just like girls, only farther down."

"You mean they sell something to make you bigger?"

"Longer and thicker. This kid saw one advertised and asked how it worked. It caused some giggles."

"They don't, do they? Work, I mean."

"Of course not. The coach told him those things are worthless and a waste of money. Maybe even dangerous."

"Where do you find those ads?"

"In magazines you'd never see. Ones with pictures of naked women."

"Do you look at them?"

"Sometimes. Guys will bring them to school. Haven't you seen ones with pictures of naked men?"

"Sure. But it's all on the Internet anyway."

"Yeah, everything's on the Internet. I think it's part of the problem. I mean the size thing."

"How do you mean?"

"Those photos always show perfect people. The women all have big breasts and the men have big, well, you know. It makes us think that's normal."

"Right. And when we don't, and most of us don't, we feel like we've flunked anatomy."

"That's how we get sucked into buying stuff that doesn't work."

"Don't forget diet plans," Eve said. "And all the fashion models who make us feel we're fat when their shots have been photoshopped."

I couldn't help laughing. "It's a screwed-up world. We're all uptight about how we look to the other sex."

"It'd be funny if it weren't so sad. Some women even have surgery to look sexier."

"It all comes down to sex. Trying to attract our opposites."

"Yeah. That won't change. It's woven into our DNA."

"Survival of the species," I said. "That's how biology books put it."

"Our programming works too well. The Earth's got more people than it can handle."

"True. I worry when I think about it."

"It can't go on forever."

"Yeah. Civilization will collapse at some point. Humans never seem to learn from history. We keep making the same mistakes over and over again."

"Maybe if things get bad enough we'll change our ways."

"It may be too late by then."

"It may be too late now."

"Thanks for the cheerful thought."

We were silent for a few minutes, splashing water with our feet, sipping our drinks, thinking our private thoughts. Mine were about Eve, and I hoped hers were about me. What I wanted was a way to take us to the next level, from friends to better friends and, I dreamed, something more.

Like a bolt of lightning out of the blue, I remembered the story Adam told me, the one from the book he read, what he used to get Marty to strip. It sounded lame, but he said she did take off all her clothes. Why should I argue with success?

The question was, would it work again? There was only one way to find out and that was trying it. There'd be some risk involved, like making a fool of myself. Worse yet, Eve might get mad, tell me to get lost and never come back.

My scheme was a gamble, but then life's a gamble. The bigger the risk the bigger the prize, or the bigger the flop. I felt simultaneously scared and excited.

"Eve," I said softly.

"Yes?"

"You know I don't have a sister."

"Yeah. You've got a little brother, right?"

"Right."

"What are you trying to say?"

"Well, it's like, you know, not having a sister, I've never really seen what a girl looks like."

"You know what girls look like. You see them every day."

"Not in the flesh."

"So, that's where you're going."

"I've seen pictures and all, like in those magazines or the Internet."

"But not the real thing, huh?"

"Yeah, something like that."

"You know what, Josh?"

"What?"

"I haven't got a brother."

She'd nailed me. Was that part in the book?

"Don't look so shocked. It's fair play. I read that book in fourth grade. The boy *and* the girl undressed."

"What book?"

"Isn't that line from *Robbie and the Leap Year Blues*?"

"I guess so."

"Haven't you read it?"

"No. Adam told me about it."

Eve gave a loud laugh. "Good old Adam. I should've

suspected he'd be mixed up in it somehow."

"He tried it with a girl once."

"Did it work?"

"Said it did. But he didn't mention her trying it on him."

"She probably didn't know the book. Not that getting undressed would've slowed Adam down. He's not what I'd call shy."

"Like me, you mean?"

"Don't put yourself down, Josh. I like a boy who's a little shy."

"You do?"

"Sure. I've got a shy side myself."

"It doesn't show."

"Good. I try hard to hide it. If you only knew how scared I was that first day in a new school."

"Really?"

"For real."

"I'm a little scared right now."

"It's brave of you to admit it."

"I don't feel brave."

"So, why are you scared?"

"About what you think of me for trying out that stupid story."

"Why's it stupid?"

"'Cause it's not me. I was trying to be like Adam."

"What would you say if you were just being you?"

"Probably nothing."

"What do you *want* to say?"

"You mean in my own words?"

"Yes."

"I'd try to get at the same thing, but without trying to trick you. That story about not having a sister's pretty dumb."

"You're right. No girl would fall for that unless she really wanted to."

"Can we pretend it never happened?

"If that's what you want."

"I guess, but where do we go from here?"

"Two choices. Go in the house, get dressed and start studying, or take off our swimsuits."

"Here?"

"It's private."

"You'll really do it?"

"I will if you will."

"Okay." My heart was beating a hundred miles a minute. "Let's do it."

Eve stood up. So did I. We smiled at each other, trying to act cool. One of us had to go first. I figured it might as well be me. After all, Eve had said I was a gentleman.

I pulled my Speedo down and stepped out of it.

Eve's eyes gave me a good going over. She unfastened her top and dropped it. Then lowered the bottom.

It's not polite to stare, but I did. Who knew when I'd get a chance like that again?

"You're beautiful," I said.

Chapter Fifteen

The whole thing lasted less than a minute, yet time stood still, frozen like a photograph of a past event, preserved forever.

That's the way we were, motionless, posing for a picture that was never made. Except etched in my mind. Every detail.

Then it was over. We took deep breaths as our muscles relaxed. Returning to life, we picked up our suits, turning around to pull them back on.

Eve broke the silence. "That was real."

"Yeah. Up front."

"Almost like little kids playing doctor."

"What?"

"You know, I'll show you mine if you show me yours."

"Oh. I never did that."

"Really?"

"No, did you?"

"Once. Preschool days with a little boy down our street. My mother caught us."

"What'd she do?"

"Nothing much. Told me I should keep my clothes on

around other people."

"It looks like you didn't learn your lesson."

"Guess not, but I don't think of you as 'other people.'"

"Thanks. What would your mom say if she'd caught us today?"

"More than she did back then. It's different now."

"I know. There's much more to see."

We both broke up, laughing harder than we ever had. Our laughter cut through the tension, bringing us back to where we'd been before. We went inside, dressed and, as I said goodbye at the door, Eve put a hand on my shoulder.

"Do you remember when Adam kissed me?"

"How could I forget? I was jealous as heck."

"I told you then if I wanted a kiss I'd ask for one."

"Those were your words."

"Well, I want one. Now."

There was nothing to say to a request like that, and I didn't need time to think about it. I simply leaned forward and put my lips on hers.

I felt Eve press against me. I put my arms around her, holding her close. I could've stayed like that, intertwined, for the rest of my life.

"Thank you," I said when we separated.

"That was nice, Josh."

"It was, wasn't it?"

"I didn't know you were such an expert."

I laughed. "Hardly. That was my first ever right-on-the-mouth kiss."

"You're kidding."

"I wish. I told you I was shy."

"Then you're a natural. You've either got it or you don't. You definitely do."

I wondered how I compared to Adam but didn't ask. I wasn't dumb enough to bring up *his* name again. If Eve said I was a good kisser, her word was enough for me.

Before I left, I gave her another kiss. A quick one. "That's a bonus for being such a good sport."

"You're something else, Josh."

"What do you mean?"

"I was still hurting from my last love. I'd decided to take it slow around boys for a while. But you're so comfortable to be with. No pressure. You make me feel safe."

"You are. Trust me."

"I do. I find myself really liking you."

"Same here."

"I know."

"So, why do you say I'm something else?"

"'Cause you sold me on your story of being shy."

"I am."

"Ha! I suppose shy boys get naked with girls every day."

"Not usually."

"How do you explain it?"

"Believe me. It wasn't a line. I was as shy as they come until I met you. I was competing with Adam. Afraid you wouldn't notice me. I forced myself out of my shell."

"All because of me?"

"Oh, yes, all because of you."

"I'm honored."

"So am I. That you like me, I mean. Can I ask you something? Something important."

"Sure."

"No pressure. I'll understand if you say no."

"What's the question?"

"Will you go with me?"

"You mean go steady?"

"Yeah. Just us. No one else."

"I'd like that."

"You would?"

"Of course I would."

"We don't have to run around telling people if you don't want to."

"I don't mind."

"You know something, Eve?"

"What?"

"You're something else yourself."

"How about another kiss?"

Tearing myself away was hard, but it was late. When I reached the street, I turned and saw Eve still standing at the door. I waved goodbye and she blew me a kiss.

Things had moved faster than I could've imagined. I'd come a long way in the last hour. Where, I wondered, to go from there?

Did I go where Adam and Amy Lynne went? Or did I just relax and enjoy going steady with Eve, hanging out together after school, going to dances and movies and the mall, hand-holding, hugging, and kissing? My thoughts buzzed like a hive of bees inside my brain.

That night at dinner I decided to have a man-to-man talk with Dad. Get his perspective. It couldn't hurt and might help.

Sure, I made fun of his light bulb jokes, but we should all be allowed one wacky side to ourselves. My father was solid and a straight shooter. If he couldn't steer me right, no one could.

Later that evening I plopped myself down next to his desk. "Dad, how many ski instructors does it take to change a light bulb?" That loosened him up as we laughed together.

"Thanks, Joshua. I'll try it on the judge in court tomorrow. It might put him in a better mood."

"Glad I could help. And, speaking of help, Dad, I could use a little myself."

"Homework?"

"Not exactly. What we talked about before."

"I see. Girls still on your mind?"

"Heavy duty about one in particular."

"Eve?"

"How'd you guess?"

"I figured you'd not give her up so soon. Not the way you talked the last time."

"Just the opposite. We're going steady."

"Congratulations. She picked the right guy after all. Where's Adam fit in?"

"He's out of the picture. Well, this picture. He's got a girl of his own."

"I'd say Eve has good taste."

"I owe a lot to you."

"For what?"

"Your advice. The part about being open and sharing my feelings. I let Eve know how I felt about her."

"Happy I helped. What's the topic tonight?"

"The next step."

"In what direction, Son?"

I hesitated, unsure how to say it. He might get upset. It wasn't what a father wanted to hear, but he's the one who said be honest.

"Sex."

"I see."

"Don't get me wrong, Dad. I'm not into that yet, but it's on my mind. I mean, I have feelings I've never had before. And everyone's talking about it. All the kids at school."

"Sex packs a lot of power for such a little word."

"It's everywhere—television, the Internet, movies, the news. You can't miss it, even if you wanted to."

"There's a saying in advertising, Joshua. 'Sex sells.' It's a basic human need. What you're feeling is natural."

"I know, but what do I do about it? I'm confused. Adam says I should go for it."

"What do you think?"

"That I want to. Bad. In our sex ed classes all they talk about is waiting."

"You mean abstinence?"

"Yeah. But for how long?"

"That depends."

"What's funny is they tell us not to do it, and then they explain about birth control and disease prevention like they know we won't wait but do it anyway."

"A mixed message?"

"Yeah. Our bodies have a foot on the accelerator and they tell us to slam on the brakes."

"You've raised a good question. It deserves a good answer."

"That's why I came to you."

"I'm glad you did. You can talk to me about anything."

"So?"

"Good news and bad news. There's not a simple solution to the spot you're in."

"Give me the good news first."

"Okay. The good news is it's up to you. Only you can decide when it's right."

"And the bad news?"

"That it all depends on you. The decision is yours alone."

"They sound a lot alike."

"That's because they are. Exactly alike. I said it wasn't simple."

"Are you saying that whatever I decide is right?"

"No, I'm not saying that."

"Then what?"

"Be informed. Know the facts. That's what the school is trying to do. Talk to people you respect. Listen carefully to what they have to say. Then sort it all out for yourself and come up with an answer you're comfortable with. In the end, you're the one who has to live with your decision."

"I think I see where you're leading."

"There's a philosophical saying that speaks to this. 'No one can take a bath for you.'"

"Weird."

"Perhaps. But true nonetheless."

"So, Dad, give me your best brainpower on the subject of sex."

"Let me start with a little history."

I laughed. "Sex or social studies?"

"A little of both."

"Okay, give it to me."

"Two forces are at work on you, Joshua. Society and biology. Each has its own agenda, so they have to be balanced."

"Trade-offs?"

"You can put it that way. The pressure you feel is from being squeezed between the two. Your body says you're a man and society says you're a child. In the past those two things were closer together. Boys your age were working and going to war. They married early. Life spans were shorter. Everything got speeded up."

"What changed?"

"Society. Jobs changed. Kids couldn't learn everything they needed at home anymore. They went to school and, as work required greater and greater skills, their school years increased. Many students today aren't prepared to join the workforce until their twenties."

"But our bodies stayed the same, right?"

"Right."

"What a mess."

"In a way. Society says sex waits for marriage, and marriage waits for you to get a good job to support a family, and a good job waits for education and training. But your body says, 'I don't want to wait.'"

"Why should it?"

"Hold that question. There's more."

"I figured there would be."

"Not that long ago, sex almost always meant babies."

"But now we have birth control."

"Yes, and generally very effective. But not foolproof. And pregnancy introduces tough choices that will affect the rest of your life."

"I know. We talked about them in class. Don't forget, I had to take care of Scott for awhile."

"Scott was the tip of the iceberg. Caring for him is nothing to decisions on birth or abortion, financial costs, delaying higher education, and many more you can't foresee."

I smiled. "Is that all?"

"Oh, no. There are some serious diseases associated with sex."

"We've studied them."

"Then you know the risks. There's no such thing as safe sex. Only safer sex. Abstinence is the only one with a guarantee."

"Yeah, but it's the hardest."

"Not compared to death."

"You've got me there."

"One more thing, Joshua."

"Yes?"

"Sex isn't only physical. It's also mental and emotional. Strong feelings come with it. Maturity helps you handle them."

"When does this maturity kick in?"

"At different times for different people. You're bright and responsible. You'll know when it's right for you if you listen to reason as much as your body. You're young, Joshua. Relax and enjoy dating. You've got plenty of time for the rest of it."

"I suppose."

"Sex is very special. It's more than mere biology. It means more with someone you love and respect."

"I can buy that."

"Believe it or not, I faced the same choices now facing you."

"You were a teenager?"

"Hard to believe, huh?"

"How'd you deal with it?"

"It was tough. I won't pretend it wasn't. But I waited. Then I met your mother and I've never regretted it."

"Thanks, Dad."

"Anytime."

I went to my room. While I remained awake, I thought of what Dad said. But my dreams were filled with other things. Like Eve in my arms and my lips on hers.

Chapter Sixteen

The next morning I still felt mixed up. But then Dad had said that was normal. Still, the teenage hot seat was uncomfortable.

What I did find comforting was going steady with Eve. I had to stop myself from jumping in the air and clicking my heels. I felt like the luckiest guy alive.

I decided to stop first at Eve's. I couldn't wait another minute to see her. When I arrived, she was coming out the door, books in hand.

"Those look awfully heavy. Can I carry them for you?"

"What will people think?" Then she grinned.

I played along. "One of two things. Either you sprained your wrist or we're a couple."

"I'll keep them. You've got an armload yourself, and this is the age of the liberated woman."

"I forgot. You're not the poor, helpless creatures you once were."

"We can even open our own doors these days."

"If you can ever get men to iron shirts, you'll have it made."

"That's probably pushing things too far. Getting men to do

domestic chores is up the road a ways."

"What do you want to study this afternoon?"

Eve looked at me seriously. "I think we'd better return to English and algebra. Yesterday's study got very advanced."

"It wasn't over *my* head. I understood every part of it."

"That's what I'm afraid of."

"Don't be scared. It was fun."

"Maybe too much."

"Can there be such a thing as too much fun?"

"There can be, if it goes too far."

"Do you think we've gone too far?"

"No, but we might if we go on from there."

"How far is too far?"

"Good question. I can't say I have a good answer. I'm wrestling with it."

We'd reached the bus stop and its waiting students. "We'll talk more at lunch. Don't lose that train of thought."

Eve smiled. "As if that's possible."

"What was I thinking?"

"You weren't."

"What?"

"Thinking."

"You're right. I wasn't. That three-letter word that starts with "s" and ends with "x" is stamped on our brains."

"And other parts, too."

"Don't remind me."

We both laughed—our own private joke. Some of the kids looked at us funny, wondering what we were up to. They could wonder all they wanted. Eve and I weren't talking.

I remembered Mom and Dad agreed on the fact that men and women are more alike than not. I wondered how true that was when it came to sex. Not the subject but the act itself. Might Eve feel the desire as strongly as I did? If so, watch out world, we might explode.

Whatever we decided, I thought it best to be prepared. Acquiring some protection was my first priority, and the easiest way was to get it from lover-boy Adam. If he came across with a condom or two, I'd be ready.

Okay, there might not be anything to be ready for. Eve and I hadn't talked our next steps through. I wondered if she'd had the same chat with her mom that I'd had with Dad. Would she have gotten similar advice?

I found Adam in the empty locker room, running late as usual. "Hey, old pal and baseball buddy. I need your help."

He gave me a skeptical, sideways look. "With what?"

"A matter of life and death."

"Sounds serious."

"Do you have an extra," I lowered my voice in case someone walked in on us, "condom?"

That took him by surprise. He didn't expect it from me, so his brain cells had to process my request.

"An extra what?"

"You heard me."

"Why one now?"

"Just in case. You never know."

Adam grinned. He could buy that. "They're in my locker.

I'll bring a few to science lab."

"Great! I knew you'd come through."

I played my heart out that afternoon in volleyball. My whole body never felt more alive. I could've boxed ten rounds with an angry kangaroo.

Adam delivered as promised, palming me two foil-covered disks as we went to our lab station.

"A thousand thanks."

"Things must be heating up with Eve."

"You never know what will come up."

"And you complain about my puns," he groaned, giving me a wink. "Don't do anything I wouldn't do."

"Is there anything you wouldn't do, Adam?"

He scratched his head. "Not that I can think of, except homework."

Even if I wanted to, I knew I shouldn't do something just because Adam did. Whatever happened, it'd be 'cause Eve and I both wanted it, now we were a couple.

We didn't have much to say on the bus ride home. I wondered if her thoughts were anything like mine. I'd know soon enough.

"I've got a chore to do for my mom before I come," I said as we stepped from the bus.

"Good. I promised my mom I'd clean my room before the city's clutter department closes it."

We left laughing and, when we got together again, there was an awkward feeling between us. It was the first time we'd been alone since we'd stripped and faced each other the day before.

We worked on English and algebra, then discussed the best way to tackle a new social studies' assignment. And, though we talked a lot, there were words unspoken. We'd reached a new level and were unsure where to go from there.

Sometimes I'd put my hand in the pocket containing the small packets Adam gave me. They pointed one way to go, the way my body wanted. But my brain gave different advice with good reasons for going another way. I listened to both sides, but my body made the stronger argument.

Ideas were fighting inside me as Eve and I paddled around the pool after our studies. If she shared my thoughts, she didn't say. We were both quiet. I finally decided if we were to get to another level I'd have to make a move.

"Eve, would you mind if I did something I've never done before, something I've always wanted to try?"

She paused for a moment, cautious, suspicious. "Like what?"

"Skinny-dip."

She laughed, relaxed at my unexpected answer. "Go ahead."

I pulled off my suit underwater and tossed it on the pool deck. I swam a few quick laps before treading water at the deep end.

"Feels great. Wish I could swim like this all the time."

"You've never done it before?"

"Nope."

"I figured nearly everyone had."

"There aren't any places around here where you wouldn't be seen. Except for private pools like yours. You can join me if you like."

"I suppose there's nothing left we haven't seen," she said, removing her swimsuit underwater as I had.

Not that we could see a lot. It wasn't like being out in the open air. Still, seeing Eve's body through the refractive power of water was sexy, even though everything looked blurry and out-of-focus.

I waited a few minutes before swimming over to the side where she stood neck deep in water. Placing my hands on the deck, my arms on either side of her and resting on her shoulders, I made a request.

"May I please have a kiss?"

"Such manners."

"My mother raised me right."

"How can I say no to a gentleman?"

"I hope you can't."

"I don't want to."

"You don't?"

"I mean I don't want to say no."

"Oh! Then say yes."

"Yes, yes, yes."

"Once will do."

I gave Eve two quick kisses followed by a deep passionate one in which our tongues touched. I wrapped my arms around her, holding her tight with her breasts pressed against my chest. I felt the beat of our hearts as an electric shock passed through us.

I released Eve, took a step back. "You think we should

do it?"

"Do what?"

"You know. IT."

"Sure I know. Why can't you say what you mean?"

"Shyness, I guess."

"Try."

"Okay. Eve, do you think we should make love?"

Silence, then, "Not here. Let's talk inside."

Eve swam to the shallow end, walked up the steps, and wrapped a towel around her. I put my hands on the deck, pushed myself up, and tied a towel around my waist.

Without a word we walked into the house and I followed her down the hallway to her bedroom. I'd never seen it before. It was wallpapered in pink flowers with a canopied bed, white and ruffled, reaching to the ceiling. I shut the door and took her hand as we sat on the edge of the bed.

"Well," I said and held my breath.

"That's a deep subject."

"What is?"

"A well. I was joking."

"Sorry, I didn't get it."

"It's not much of a joke."

"No, but love is. A deep subject, I mean."

"It is."

"So, what should we do about it?"

"I don't know."

"Me neither. I know what I want to do."

"Me, too."

"You do?"

"Sure. I like you, Josh. I really like you. More than any boy I've ever known. And I'm just as curious about love as you are. I want to know how it feels."

"It's like the only thing I think about anymore. And it's all X-rated."

"I know. Our world is saturated with sex."

"I read a survey," I said. "It said forty-three percent of kids our age have done it."

"Really? Sounds like a lot."

"I wonder if they were all telling the truth?"

"I don't know. Some will lie 'cause they want to seem grownup."

"You're probably right. But it doesn't help us. We still have to decide for ourselves." I wanted to hold Eve right then, to feel her soft skin, but I knew once I started I'd find it hard to stop.

"There are babies to think of."

"I've got a condom."

"They're not foolproof."

"I know."

"Can you see us carrying around a real, live Scott?"

"No. A bag of flour was more than enough."

"My mom tells me it's important to wait, that sex is too powerful for someone my age."

"I got the same message from my dad. He talked about maturity."

"How mature do you think we have to be?"

"I dunno. Maybe we'll know when that time comes."

"You mean we'll be ready when we don't have to ask the question?"

"Something like that."

"I think we just decided to wait."

It was the right decision, but I can't pretend I liked it.

"I feel a little more mature already," I said.

"Me, too."

I liked that Eve and I agreed. Taking her hand, I squeezed it three times.

"That means I love you."

She squeezed mine four times.

"I love you very much."

We sat there for a long time, holding hands, not talking. Sometimes silence is louder than words.

"Let's get dressed," I said, starting to feel funny sitting on her bed in nothing but a towel. I also wanted to avoid temptation. "There's plenty of time to decide about sex."

"You're right, Josh. We don't have to rush into it, even if other kids do."

"Another sign of maturity. I just remembered something, Eve. Something Yogi Berra said."

"The baseball player?"

"Right." He said, "'Baseball is ninety percent physical and the other half is mental.'"

"That doesn't add up."

"Don't you see? It's like sex. The physical feeling is so strong, ninety percent worth, that you have to make the mental part even stronger to balance it out."

"Makes sense, in a crazy kind of way. I remember something, too."

"What's that?"

"A song title. 'More Than Friends, Less Than Lovers.' Fits us, don't you think?"

"Yeah. Feels like the best way for now."

"I agree, but it doesn't change how we feel inside."

"No, nothing will do that. It's part of who we are. But we can live with it awhile longer, can't we?"

"As long as we do it together."

We dressed and met once more at her front door.

"I'm glad we're friends, Eve."

"More than friends, remember?"

"Like I could forget."

I laid a long, lingering kiss on her lips.

I don't remember walking home. I must've floated.

Made in the USA
Charleston, SC
11 February 2016